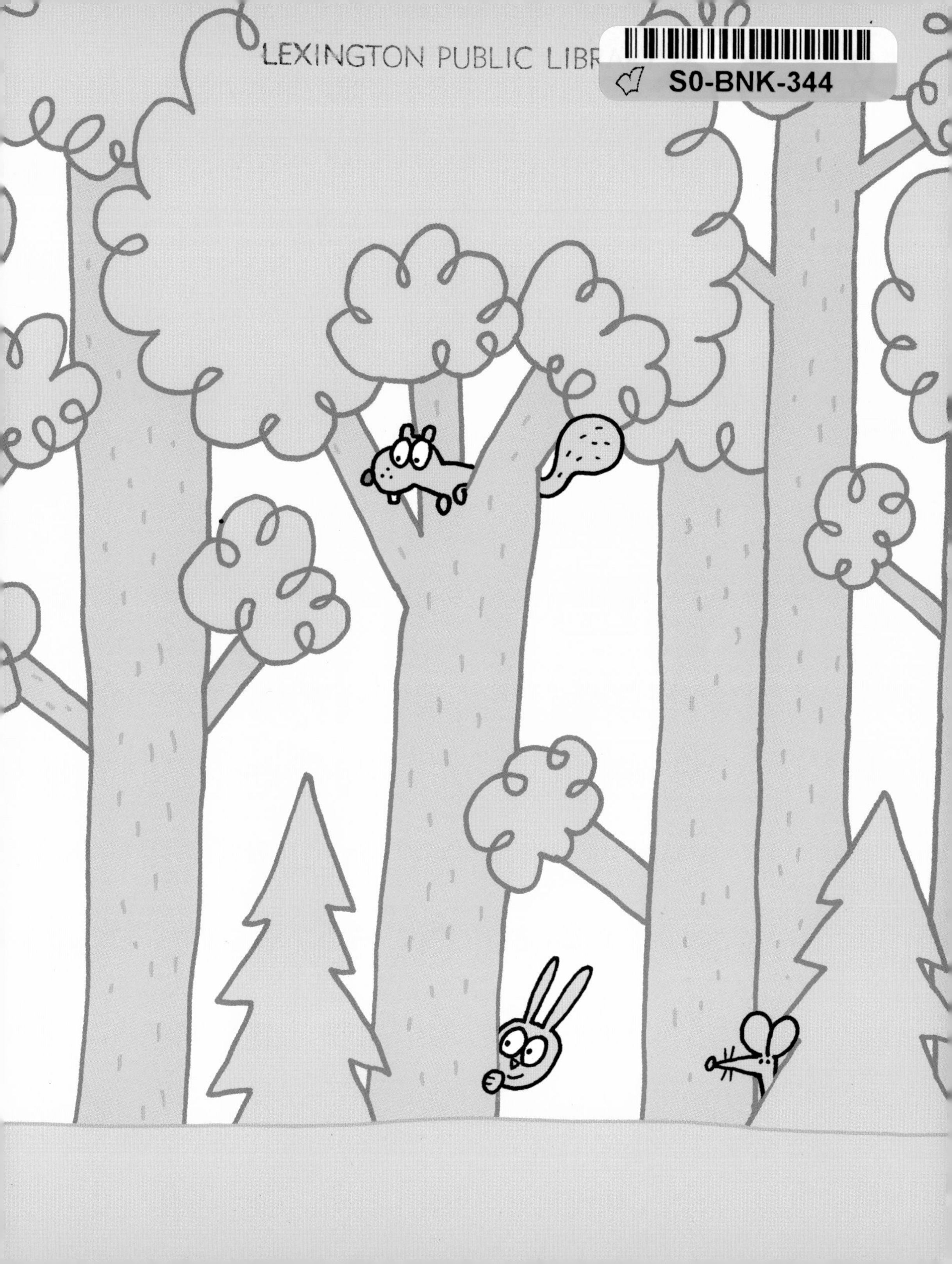

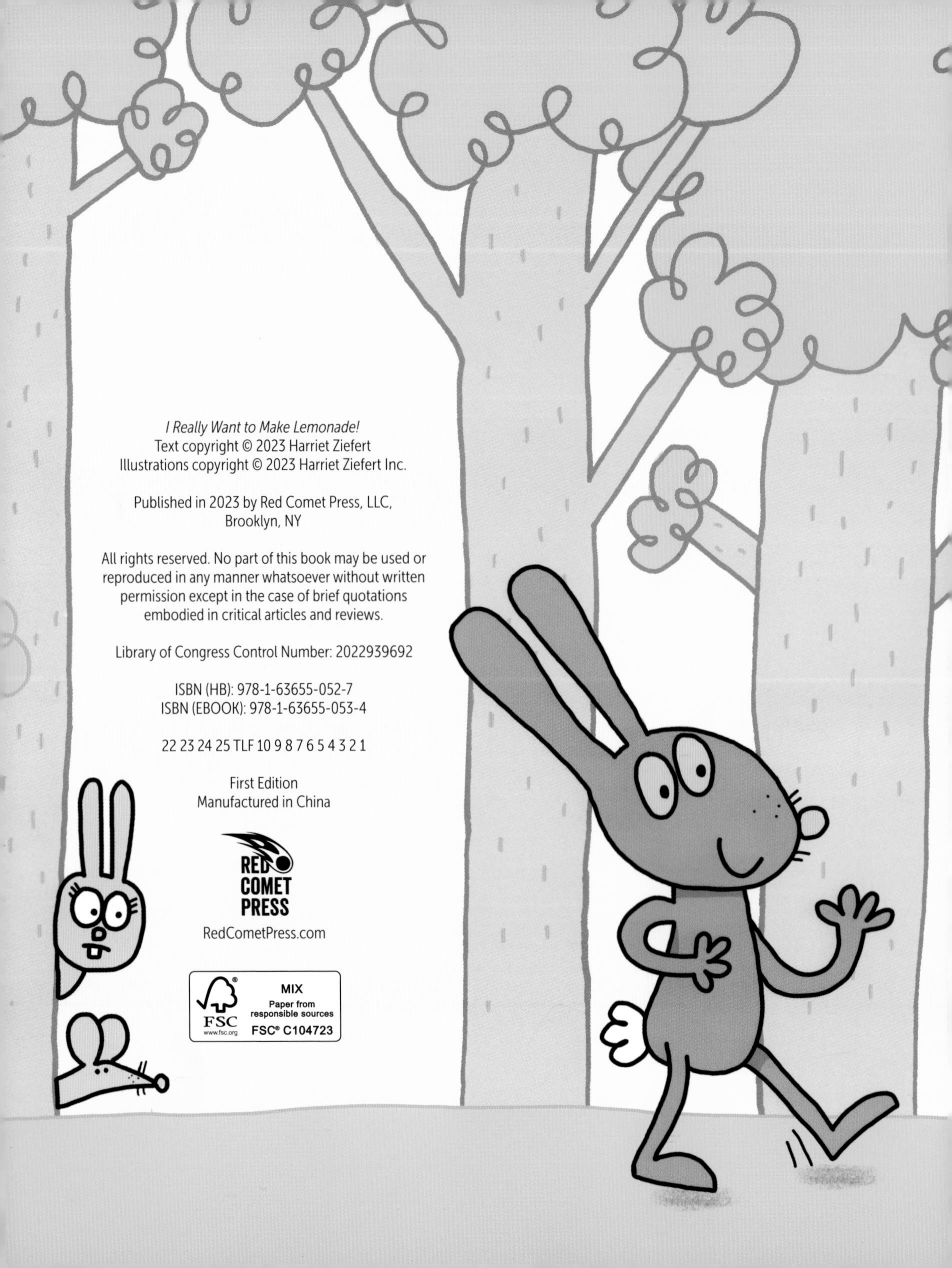

*I Really Want to Make Lemonade!*


Published in 2023 by Red Comet Press, LLC,
Brooklyn, NY



Library of Congress Control Number: 2022939692

ISBN (HB): 978-1-63655-052-7
ISBN (EBOOK): 978-1-63655-053-4

22 23 24 25 TLF 10 9 8 7 6 5 4 3 2 1

First Edition
Manufactured in China

RED COMET PRESS
RedCometPress.com

MIX
Paper from responsible sources
FSC® C104723
www.fsc.org

A REALLY BIRD STORY

Harriet Ziefert

# I Really Want to Make Lemonade!

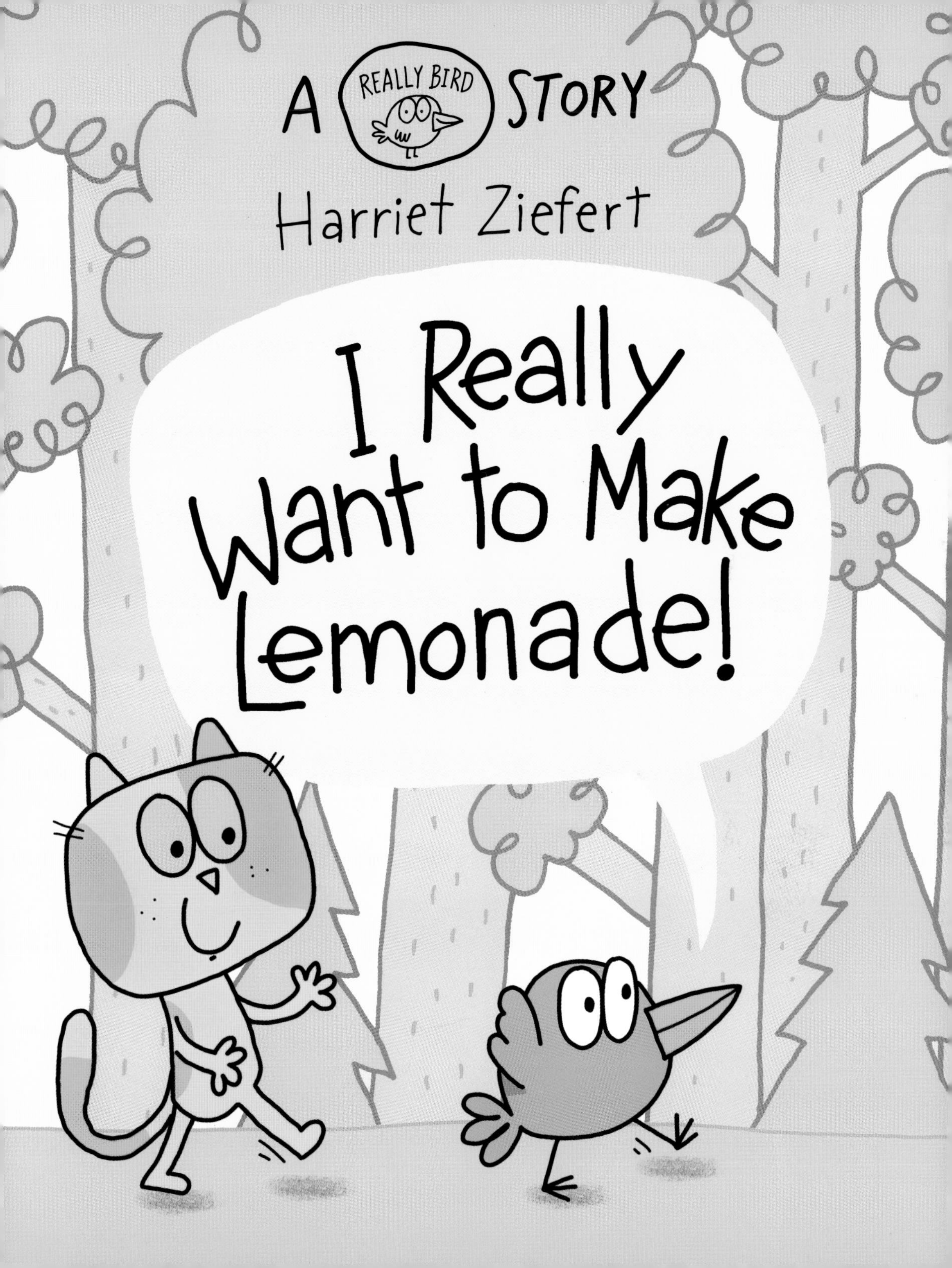

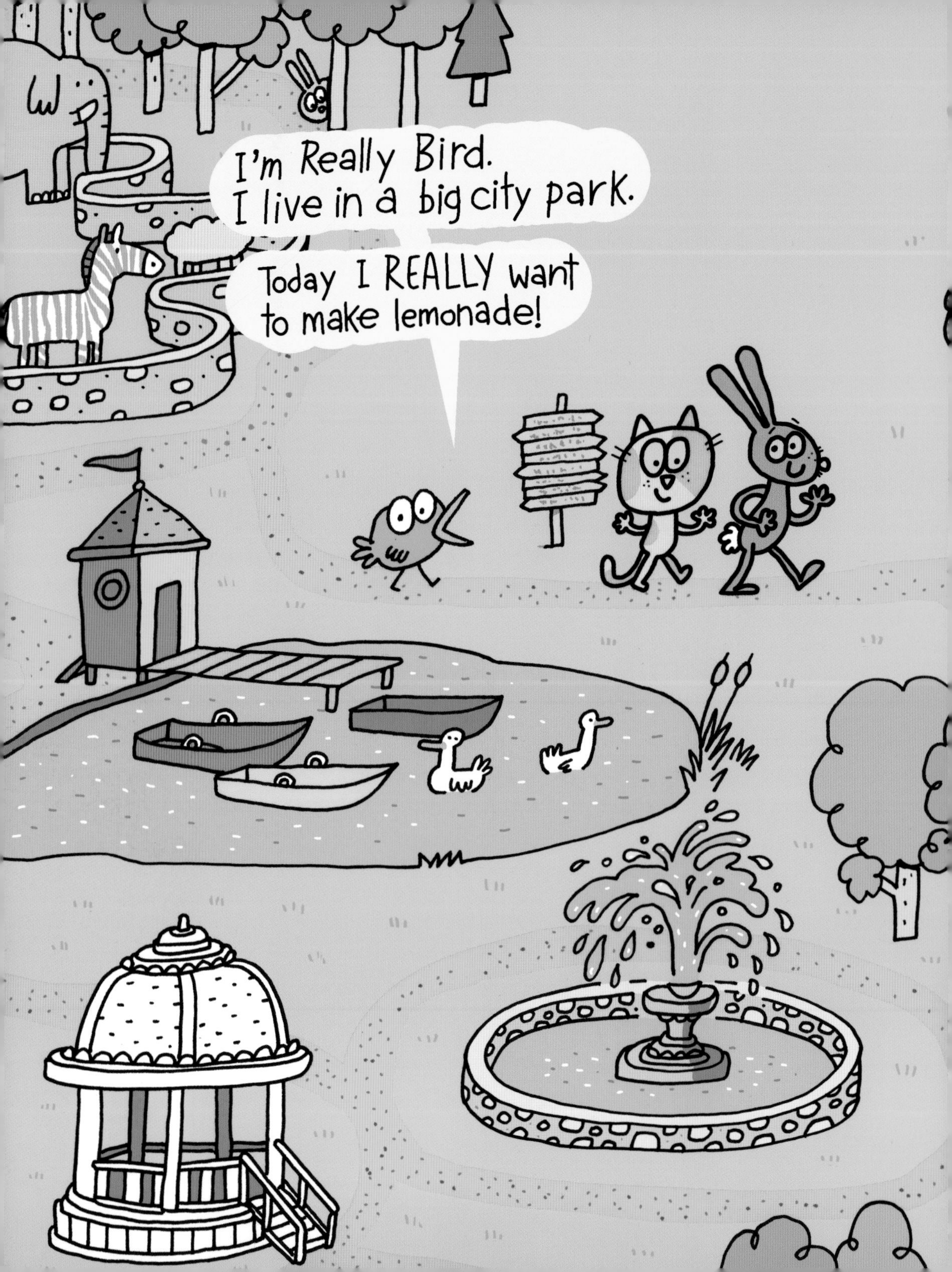
I'm Really Bird.
I live in a big city park.
Today I REALLY want to make lemonade!

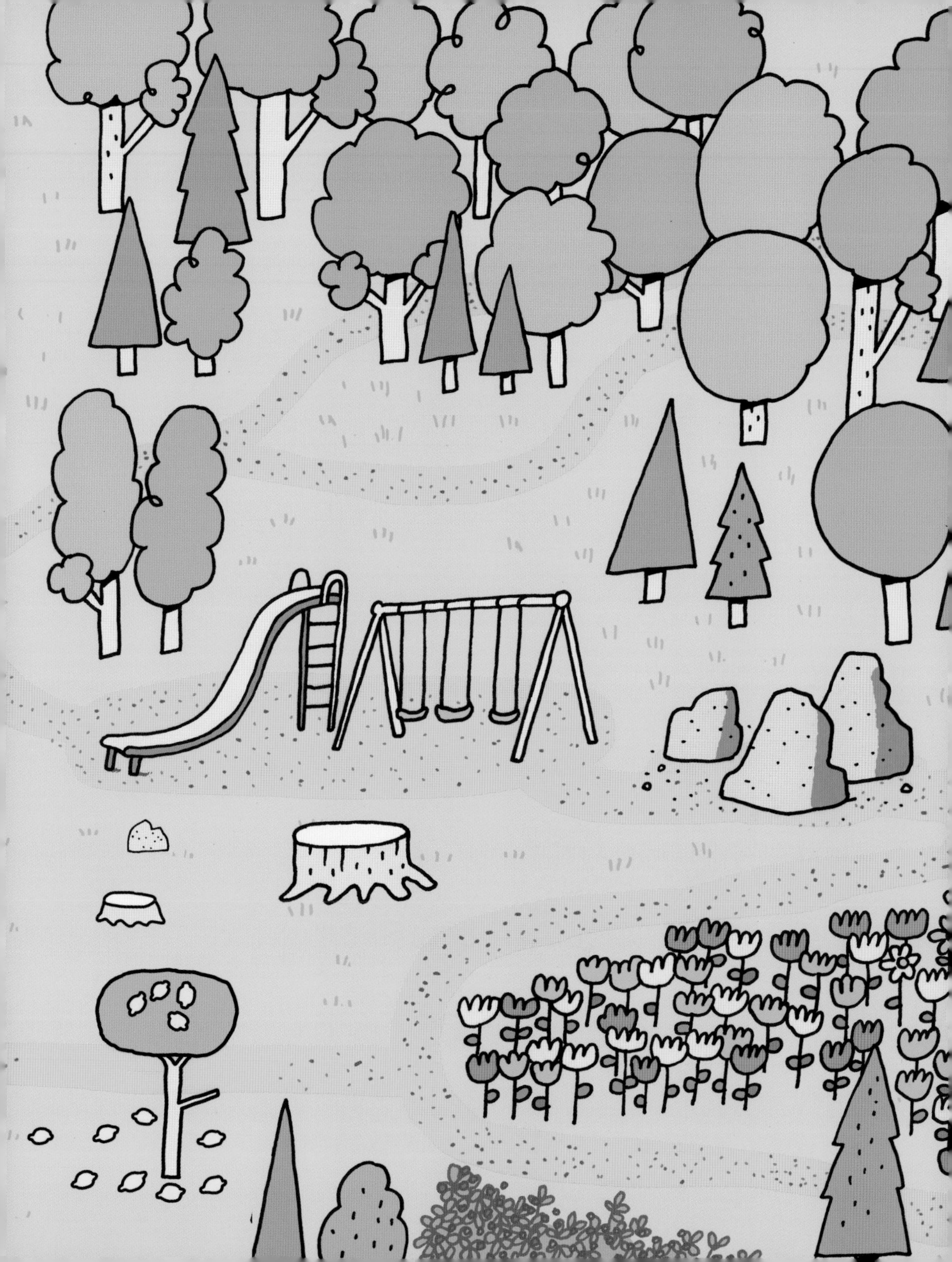

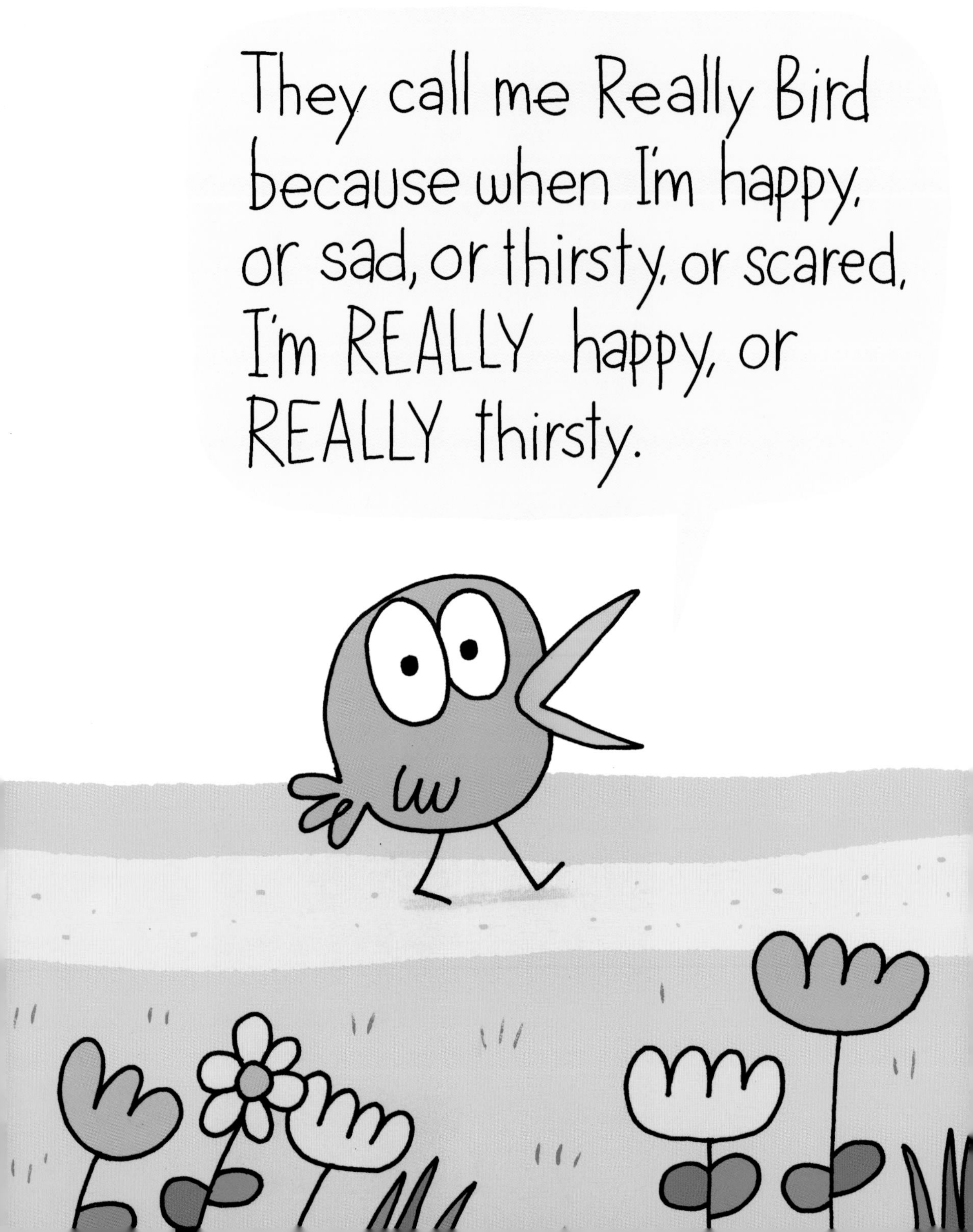
They call me Really Bird because when I'm happy, or sad, or thirsty, or scared, I'm REALLY happy, or REALLY thirsty.

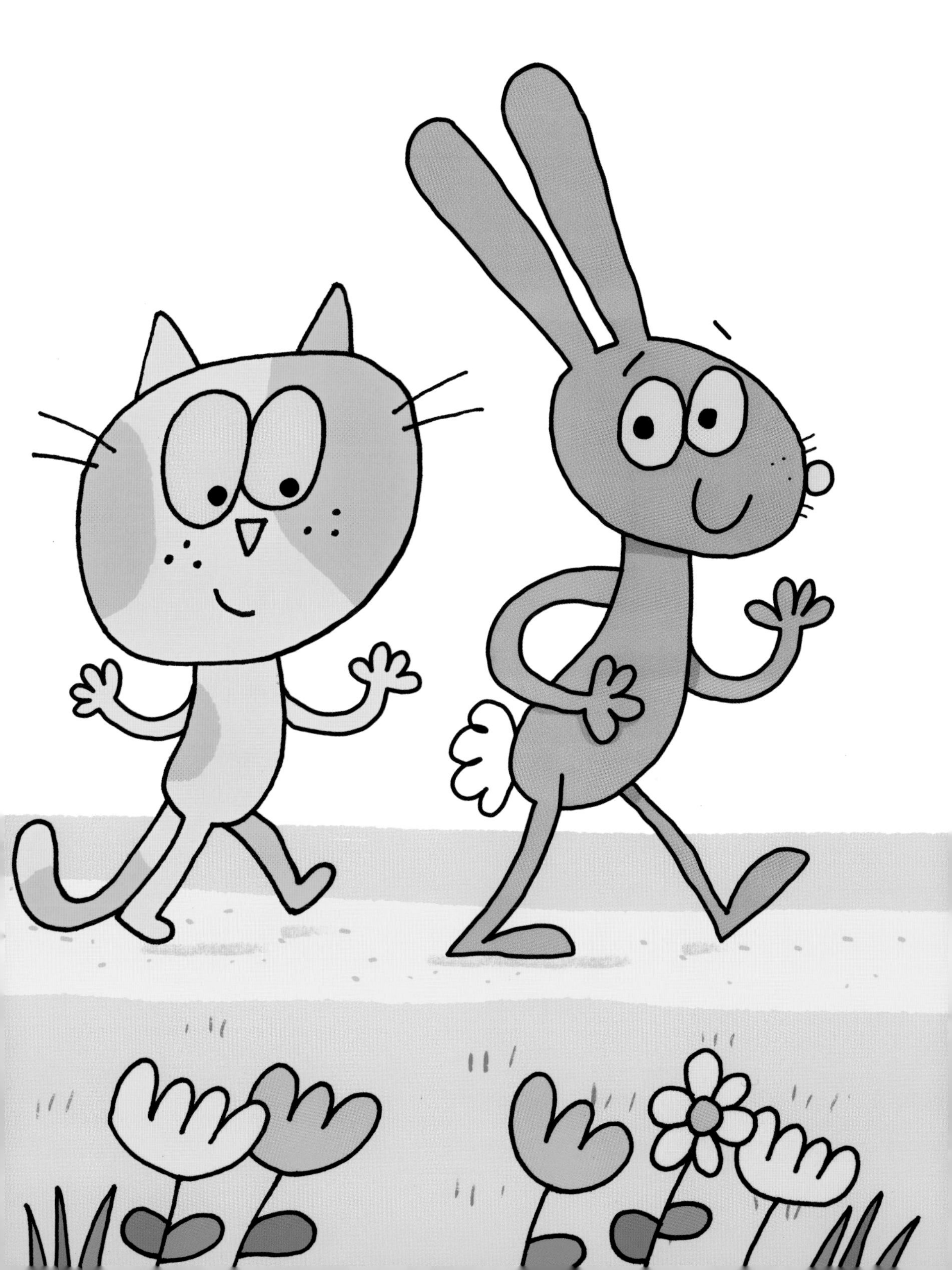

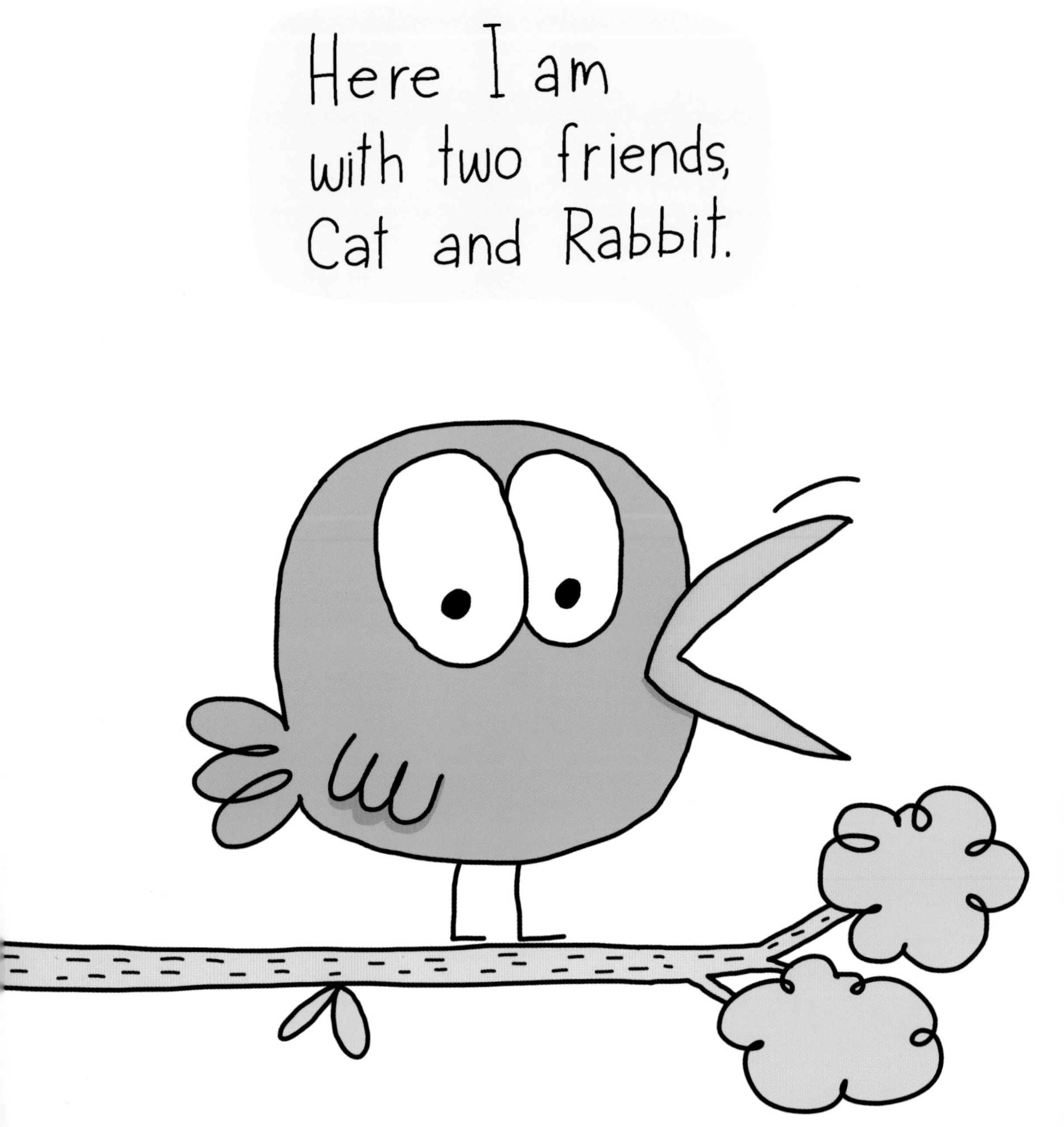
Here I am
with two friends,
Cat and Rabbit.

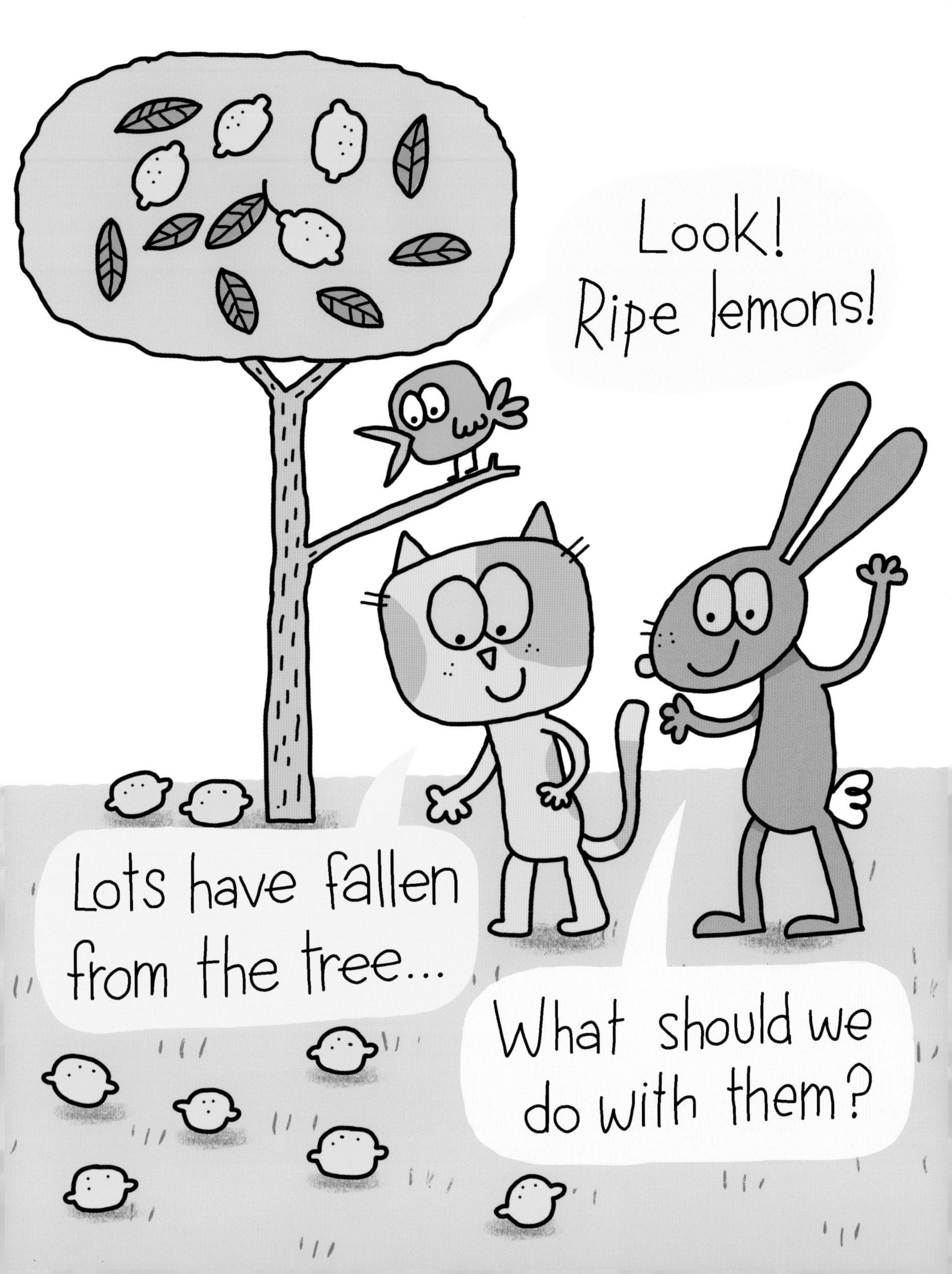
Look! Ripe lemons!
Lots have fallen from the tree...
What should we do with them?

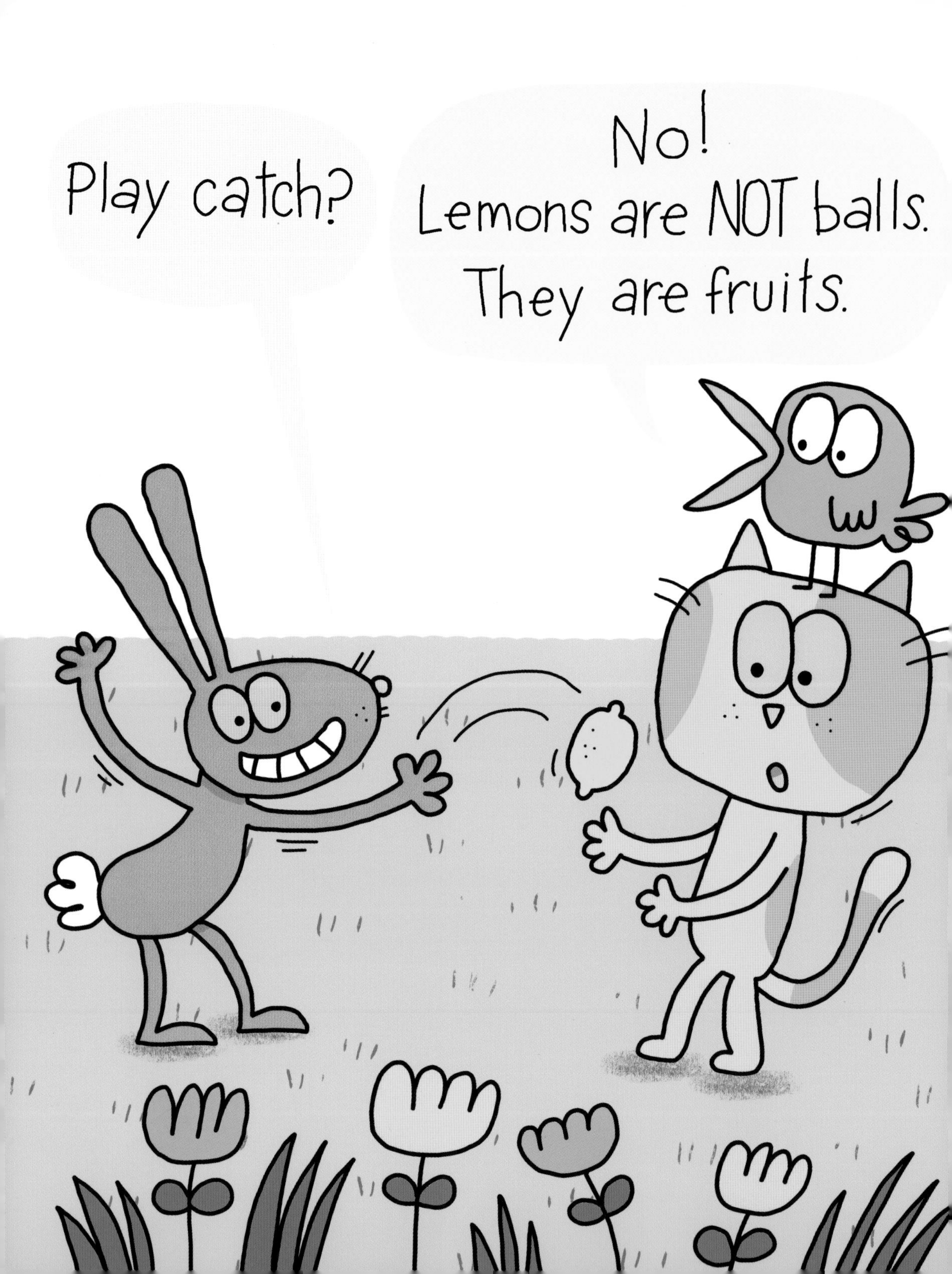
Play catch?
No! Lemons are NOT balls. They are fruits.

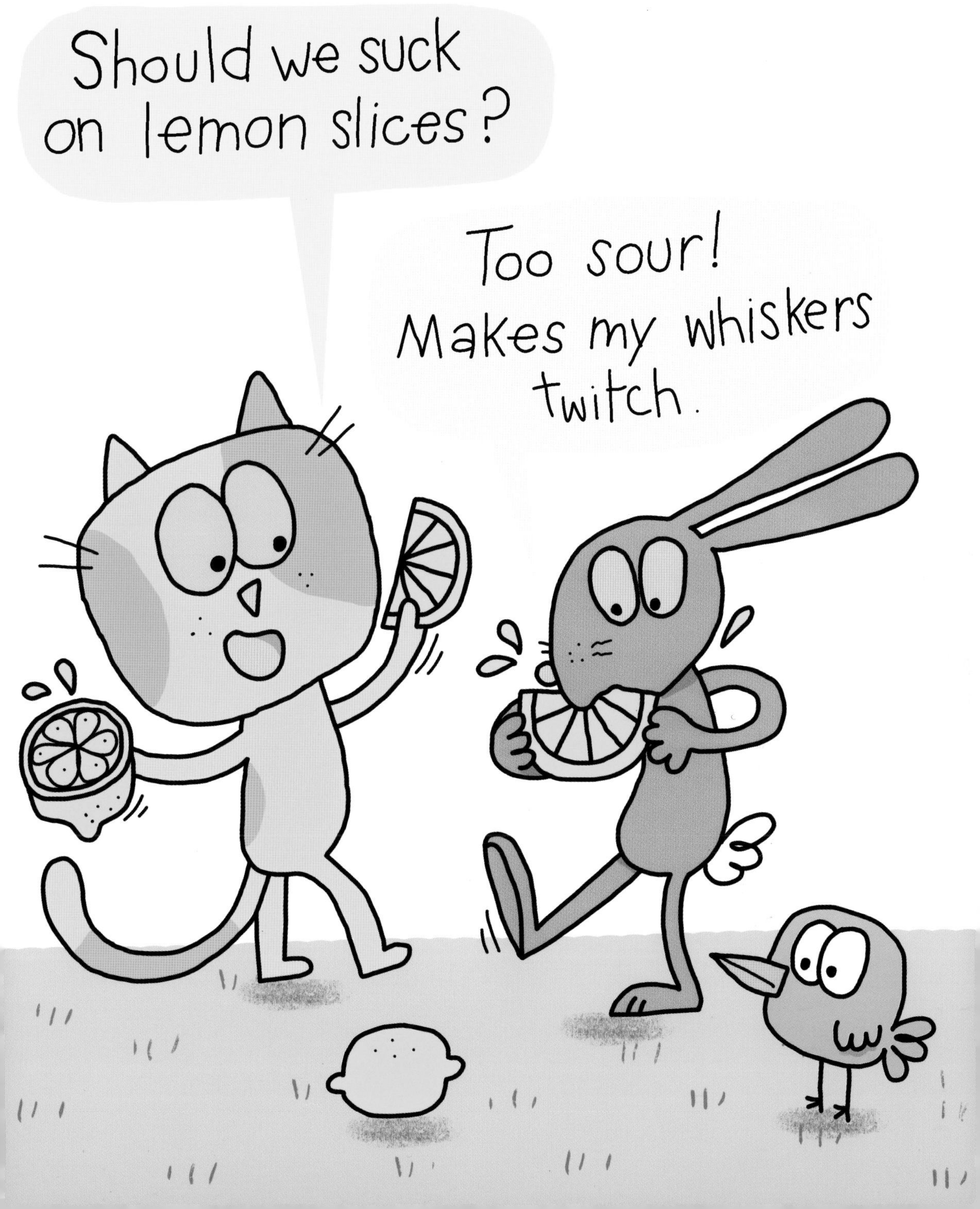
Should we suck on lemon slices?
Too sour! Makes my whiskers twitch.

So let's squeeze lemons and make lemonade!
Yeah! If life gives you lemons, make lemonade!
What do you mean?
Don't Know. It's just something I heard. But let's MAKE LEMONADE!

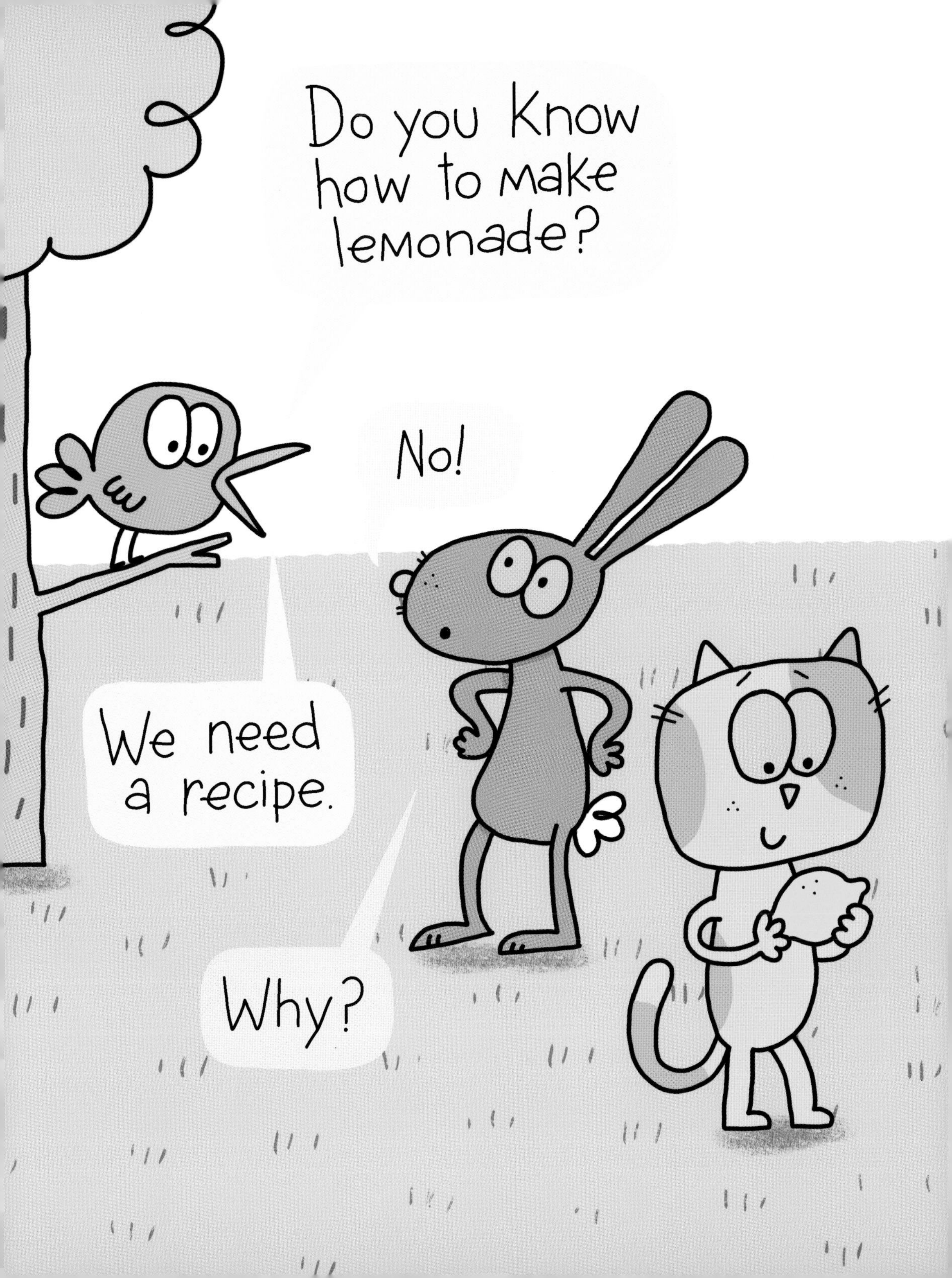
Do you know how to make lemonade?
No!
We need a recipe.
Why?

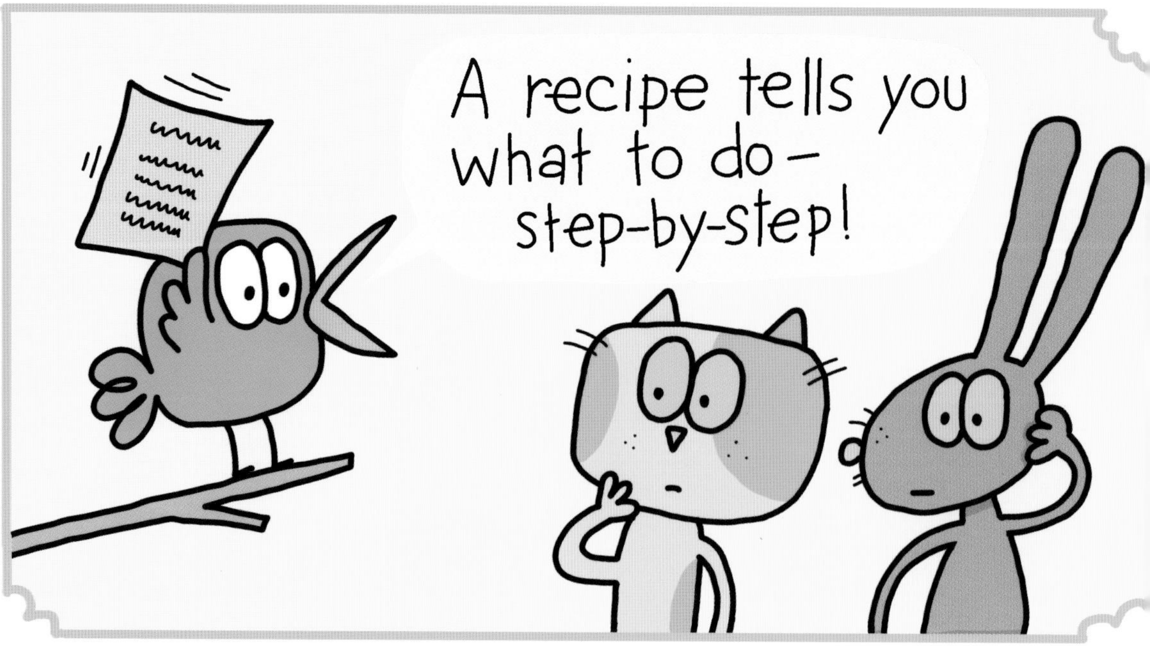
A recipe tells you what to do– step-by-step!

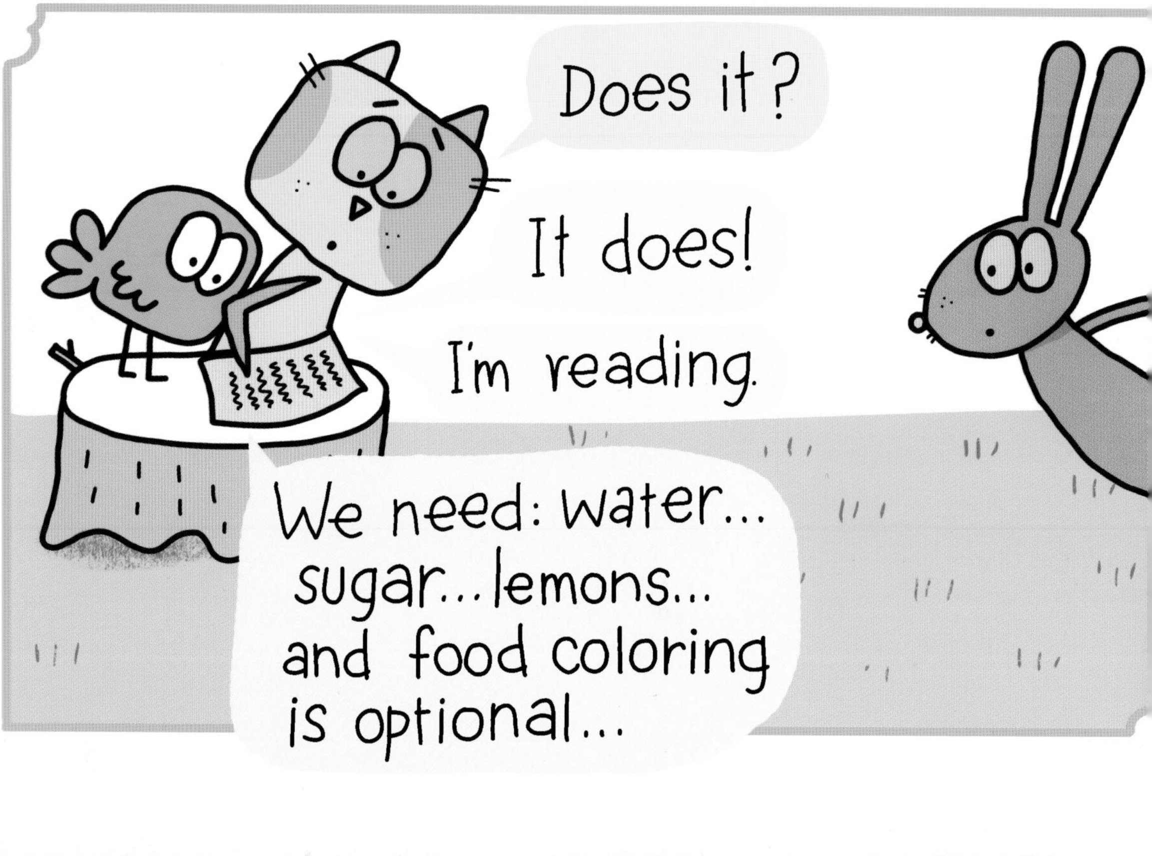
Does it?
It does!
I'm reading.
We need: water... sugar...lemons... and food coloring is optional...

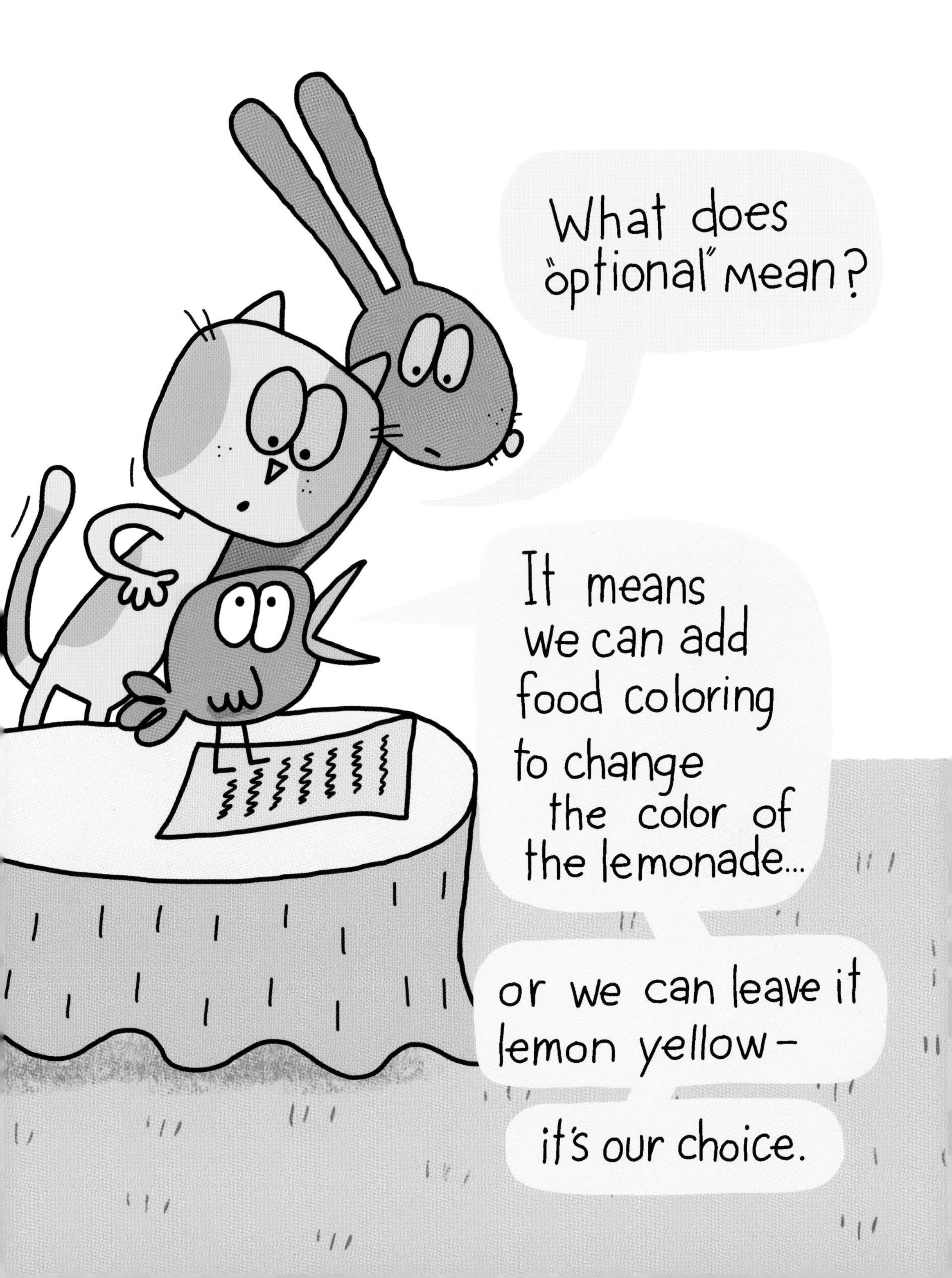
What does "optional" mean?
It means we can add food coloring to change the color of the lemonade...
or we can leave it lemon yellow–
it's our choice.

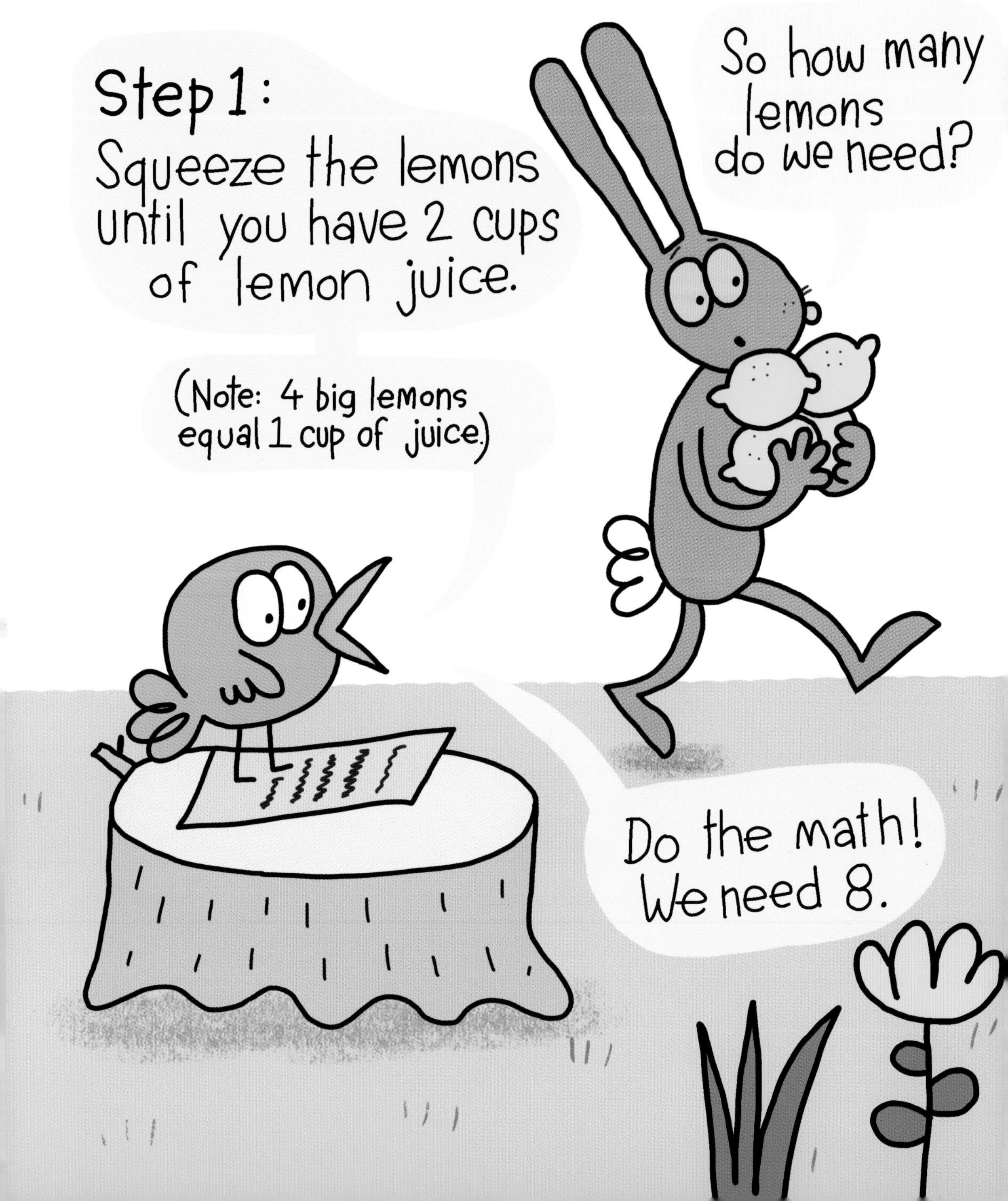
Step 1:
Squeeze the lemons until you have 2 cups of lemon juice.
(Note: 4 big lemons equal 1 cup of juice.)
So how many lemons do we need?
Do the math! We need 8.

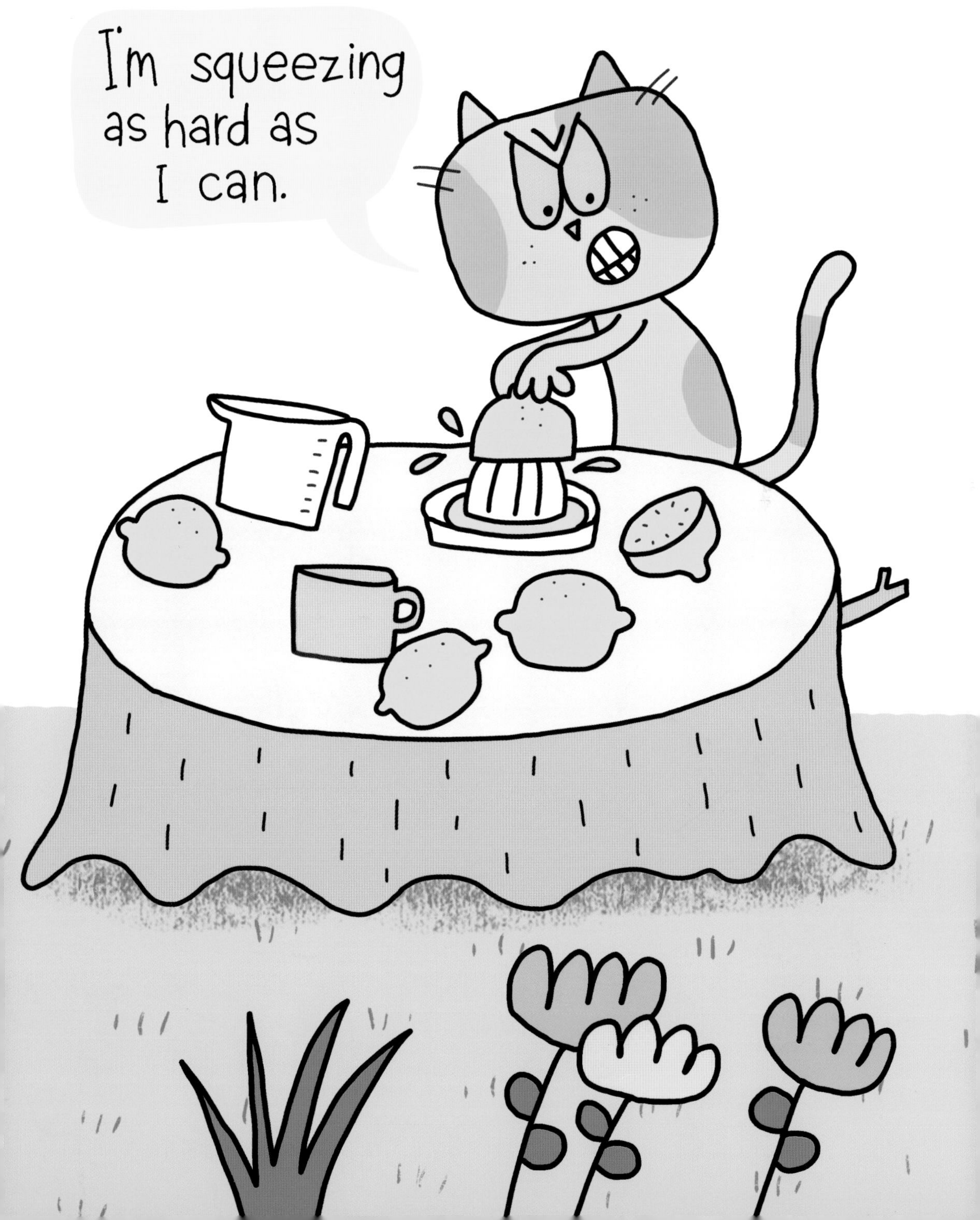
I'm squeezing as hard as I can.

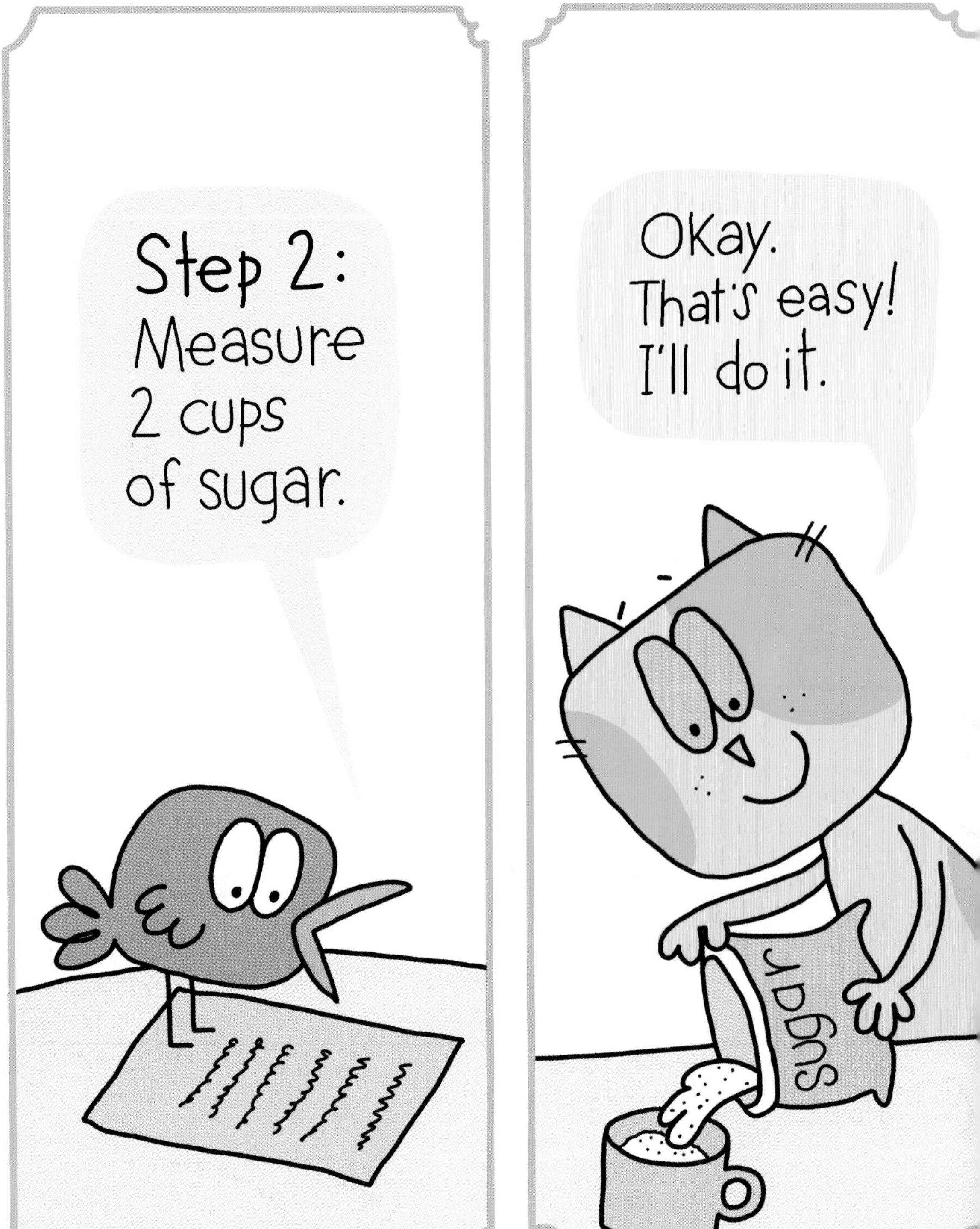
Step 2: Measure 2 cups of sugar.
Okay. That's easy! I'll do it.
sugar

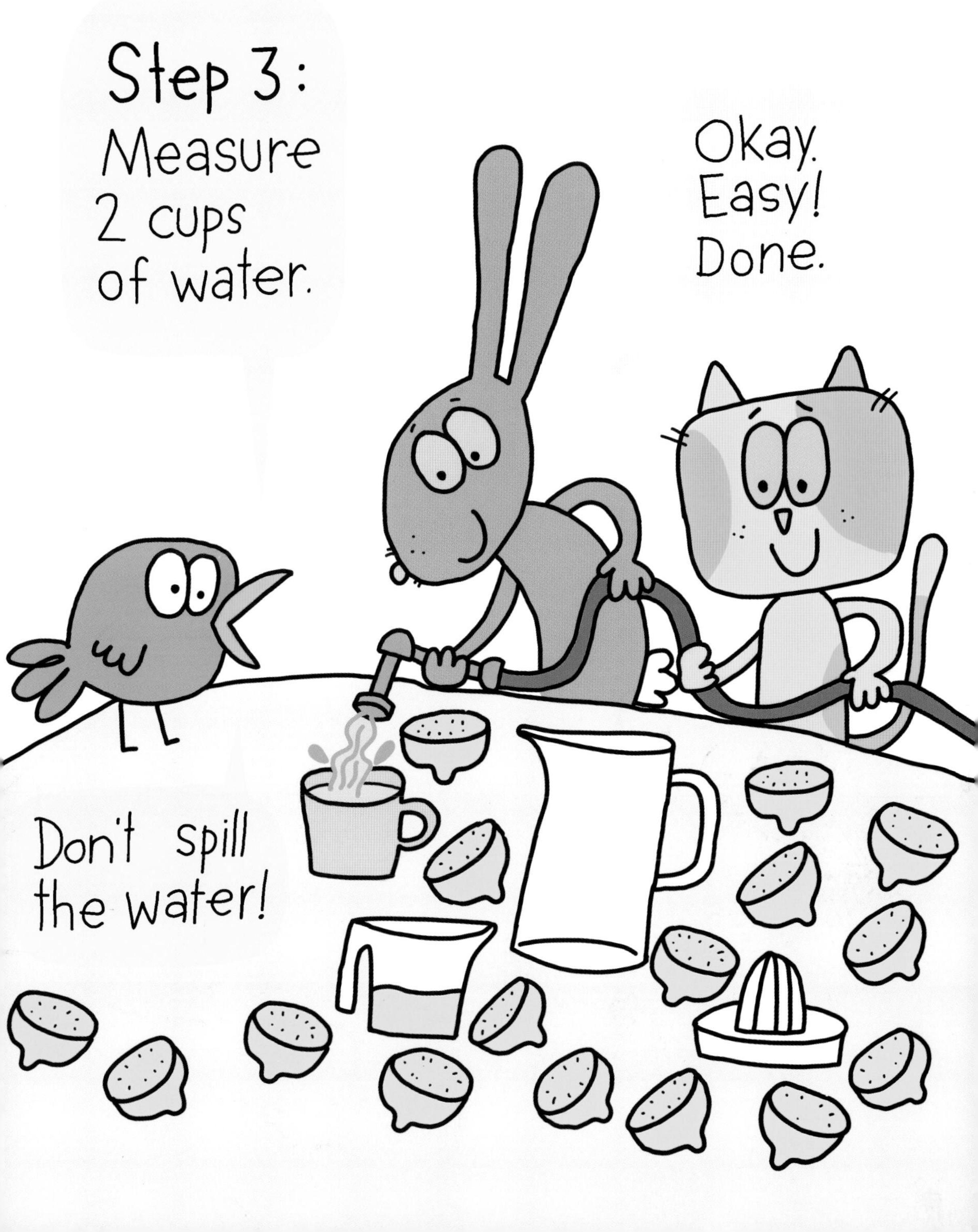
Step 3: Measure 2 cups of water.
Okay. Easy! Done.
Don't spill the water!

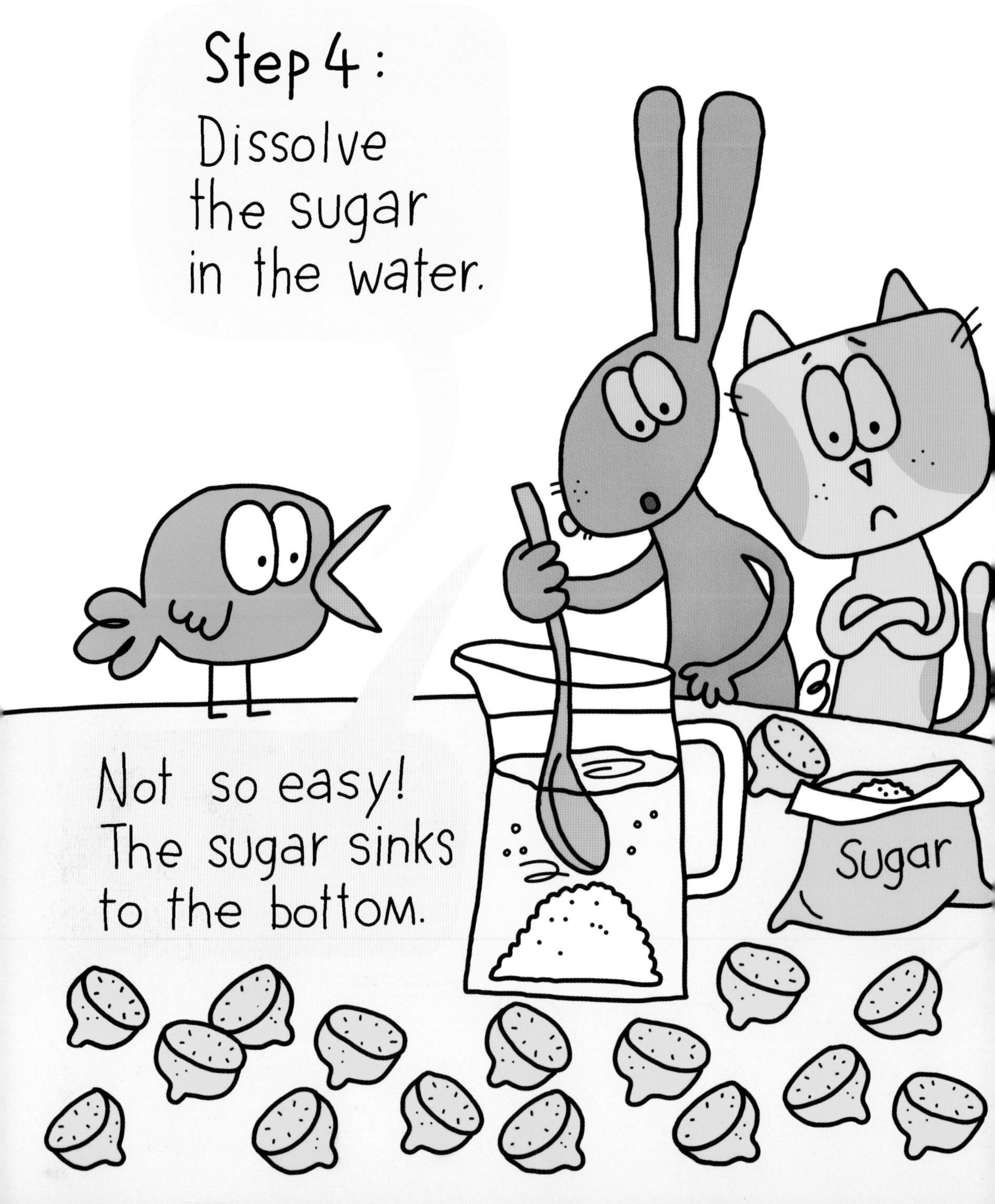
Step 4: Dissolve the sugar in the water.
Not so easy! The sugar sinks to the bottom.
Sugar

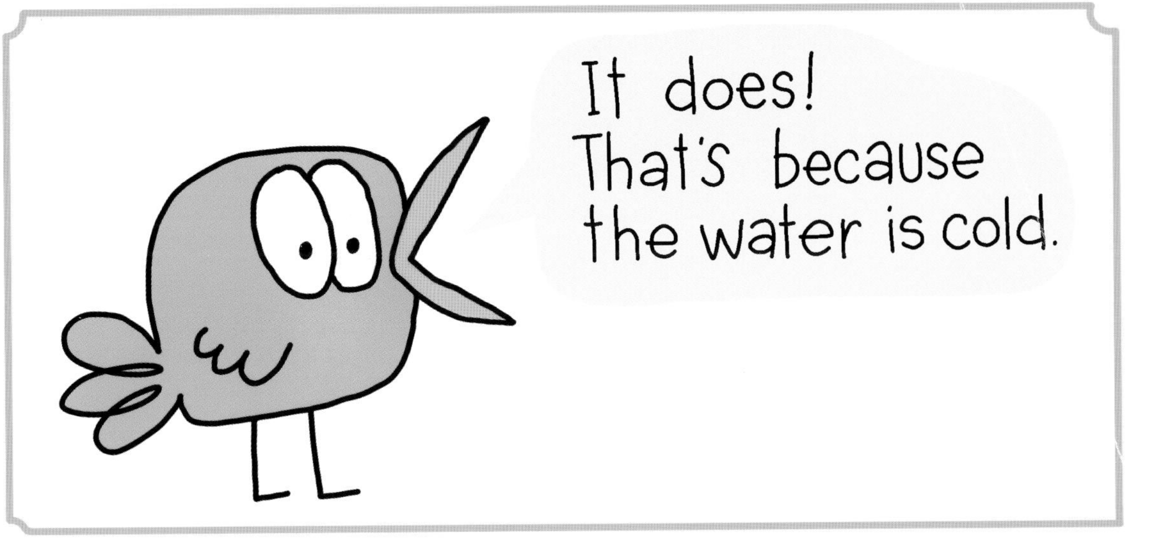
It does! That's because the water is cold.

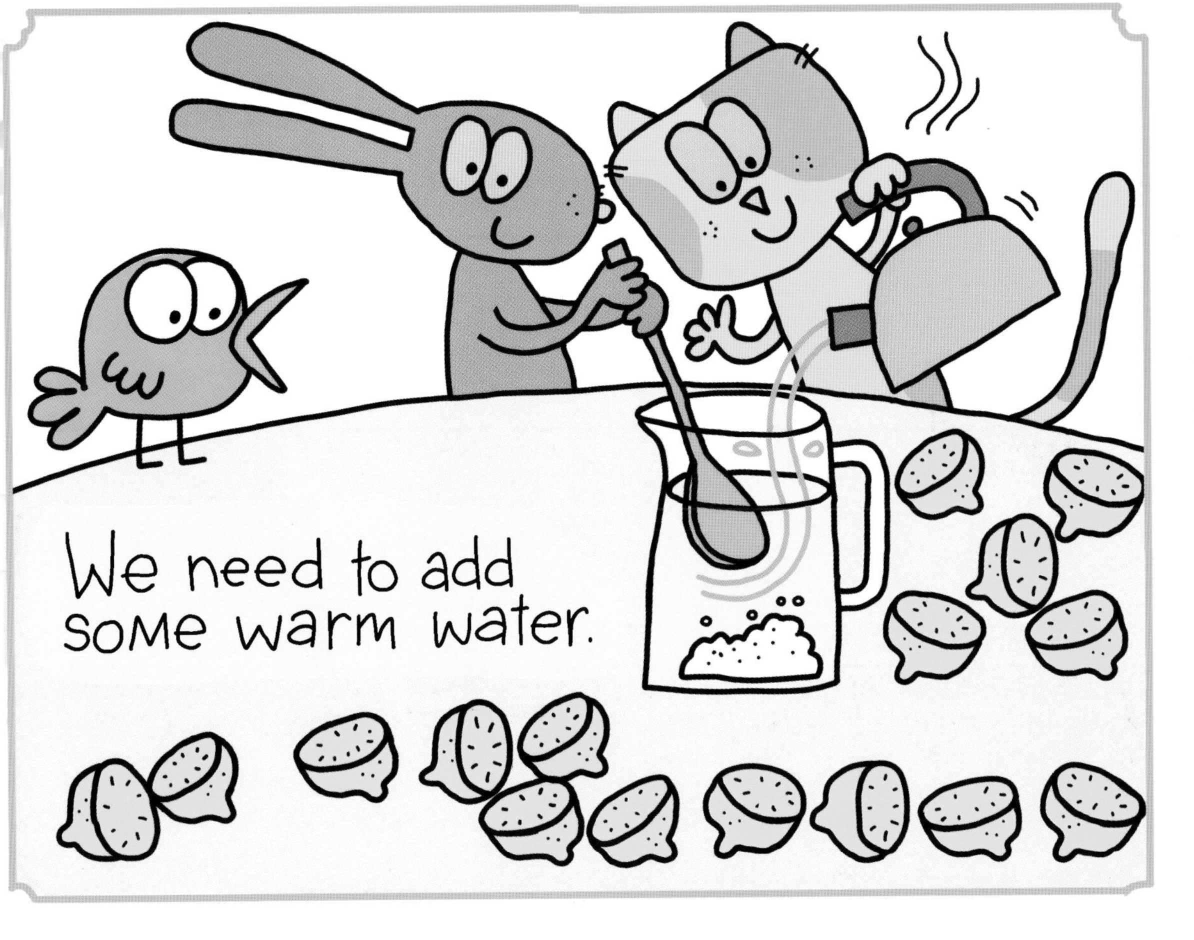
We need to add some warm water.

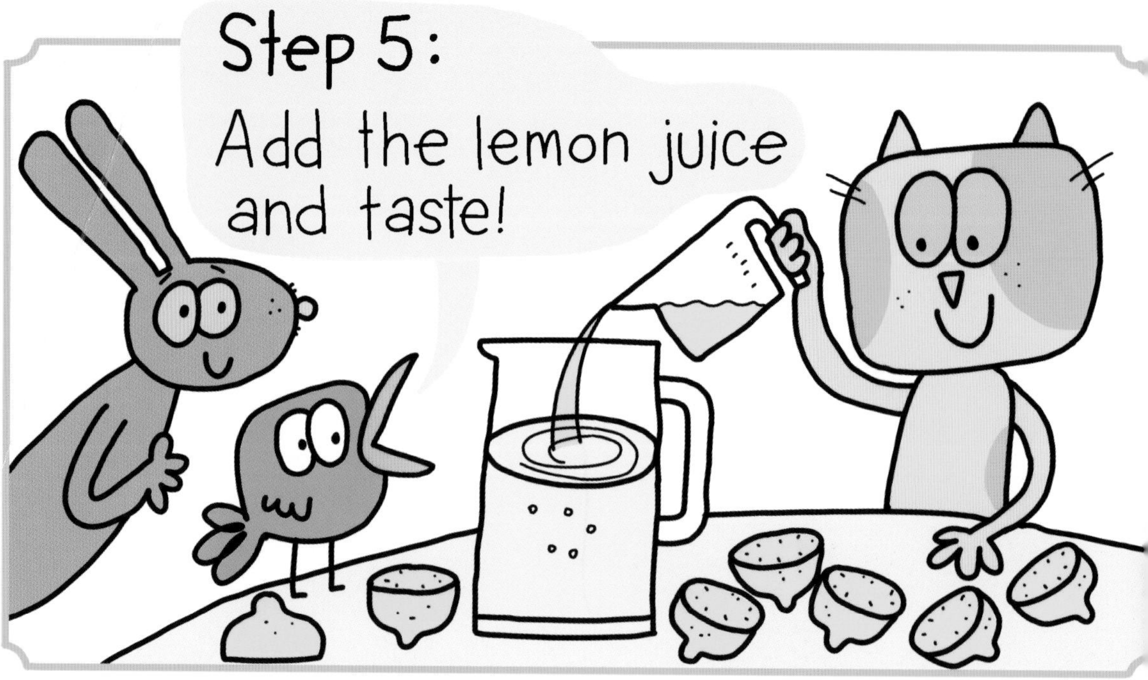
Step 5:
Add the lemon juice and taste!

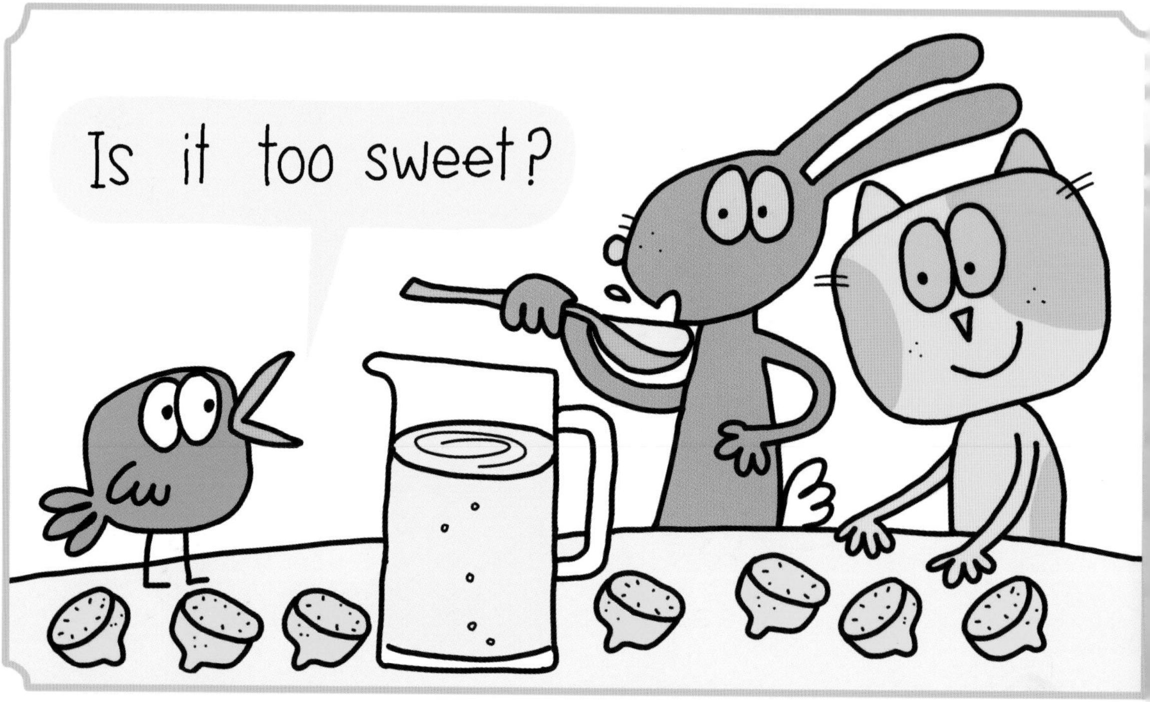
Is it too sweet?

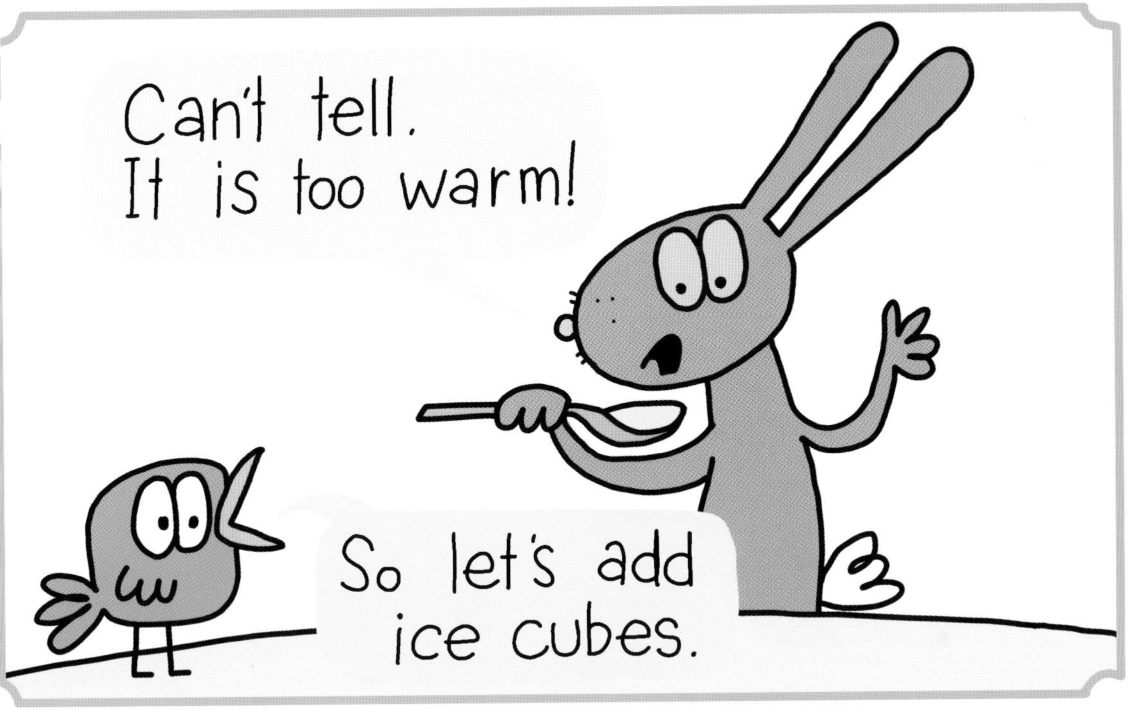
Can't tell.
It is too warm!
So let's add
ice cubes.

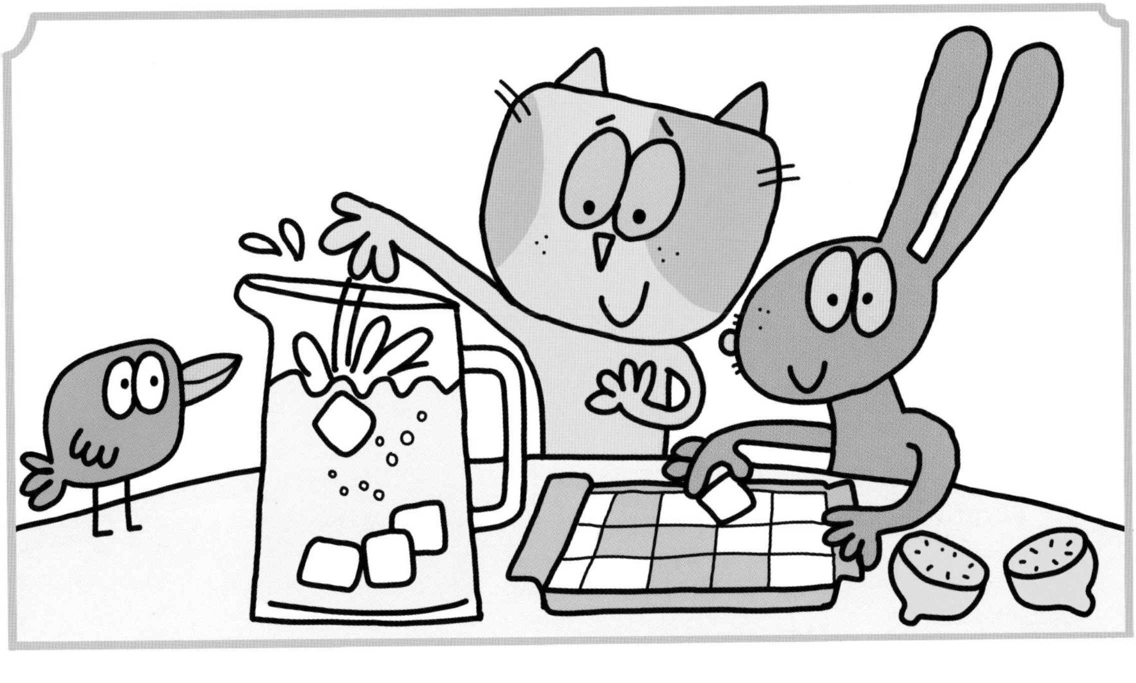

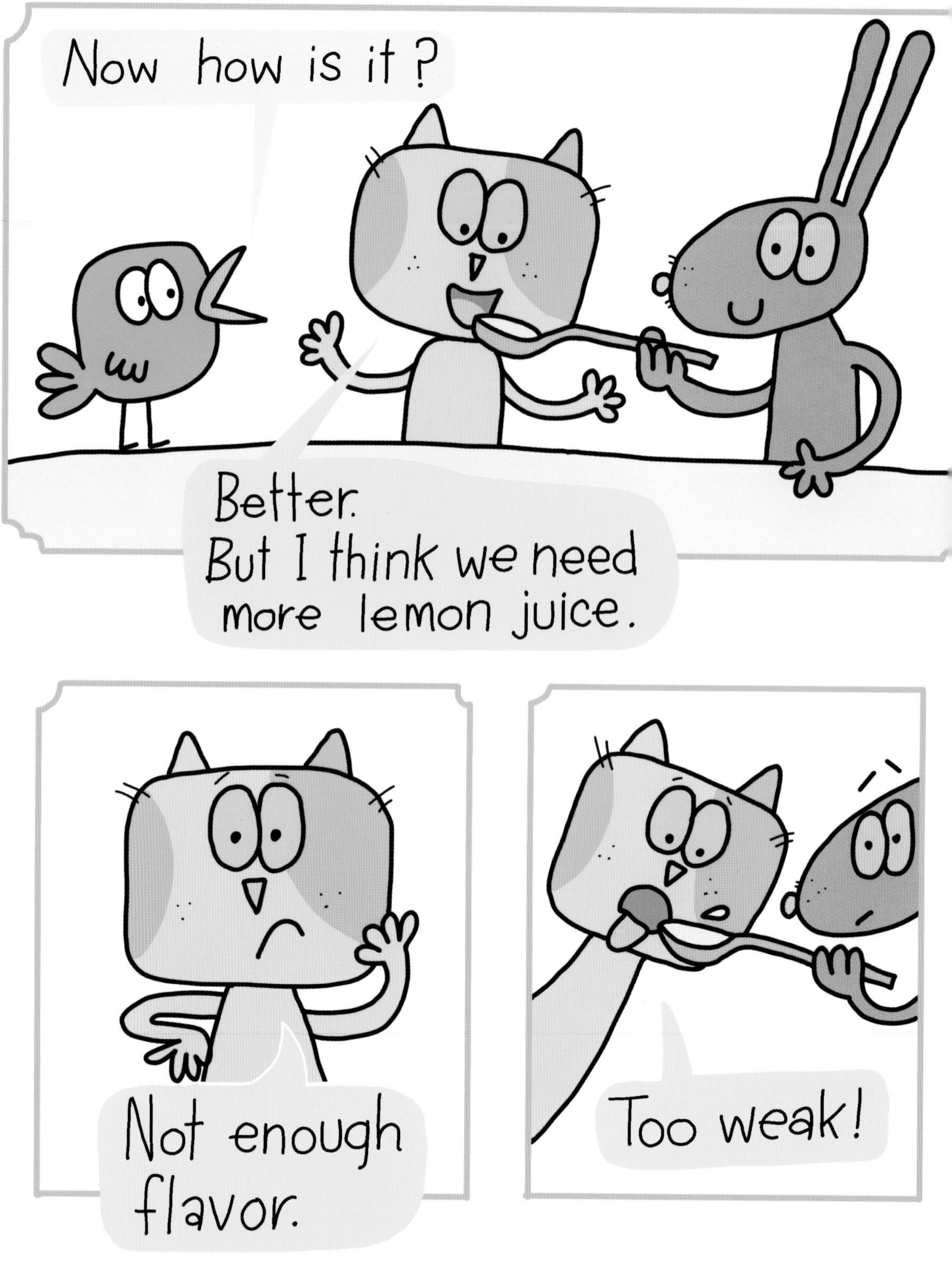
Now how is it?
Better. But I think we need more lemon juice.
Not enough flavor.
Too weak!

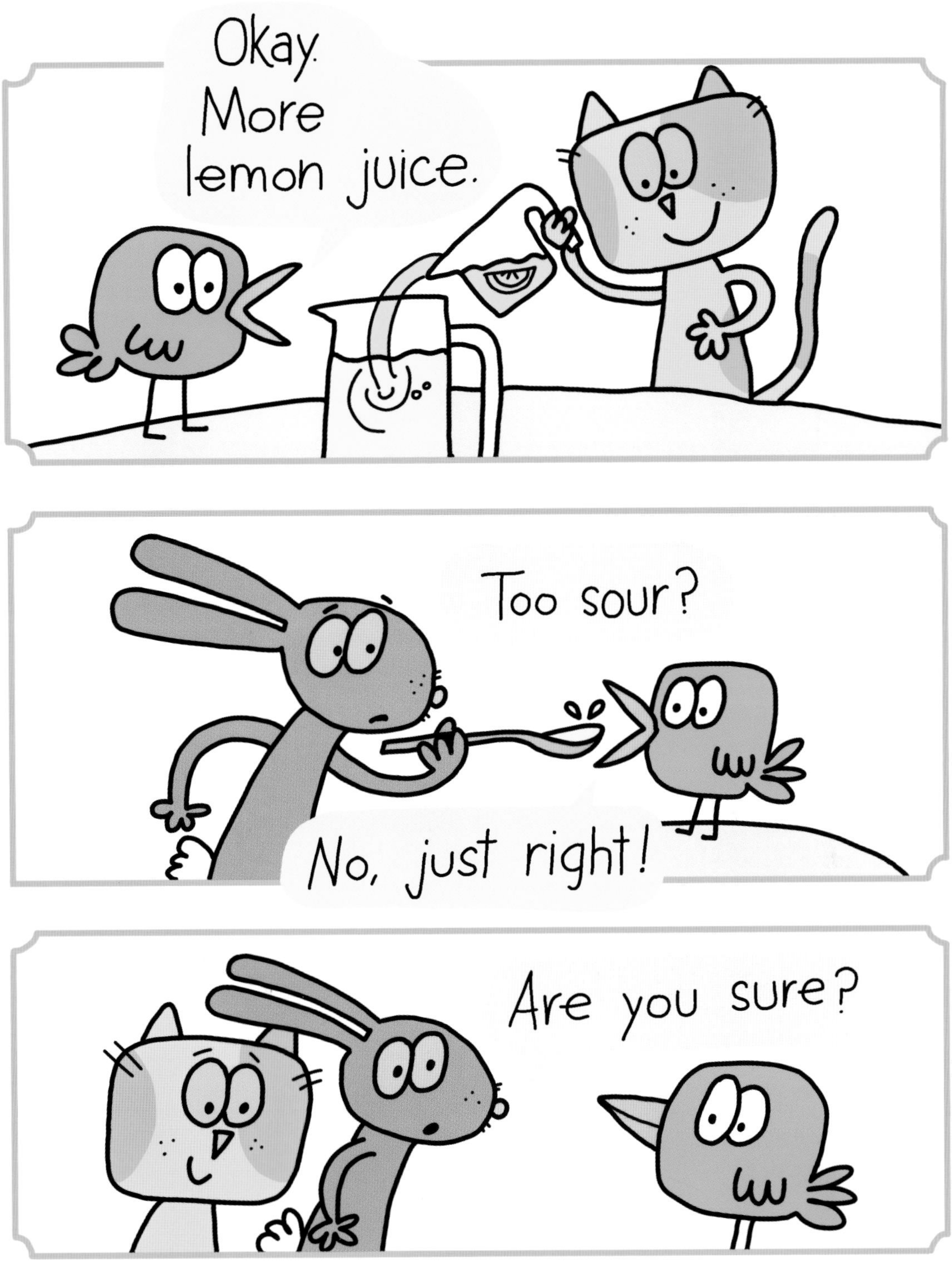
Okay. More lemon juice.
Too sour?
No, just right!
Are you sure?

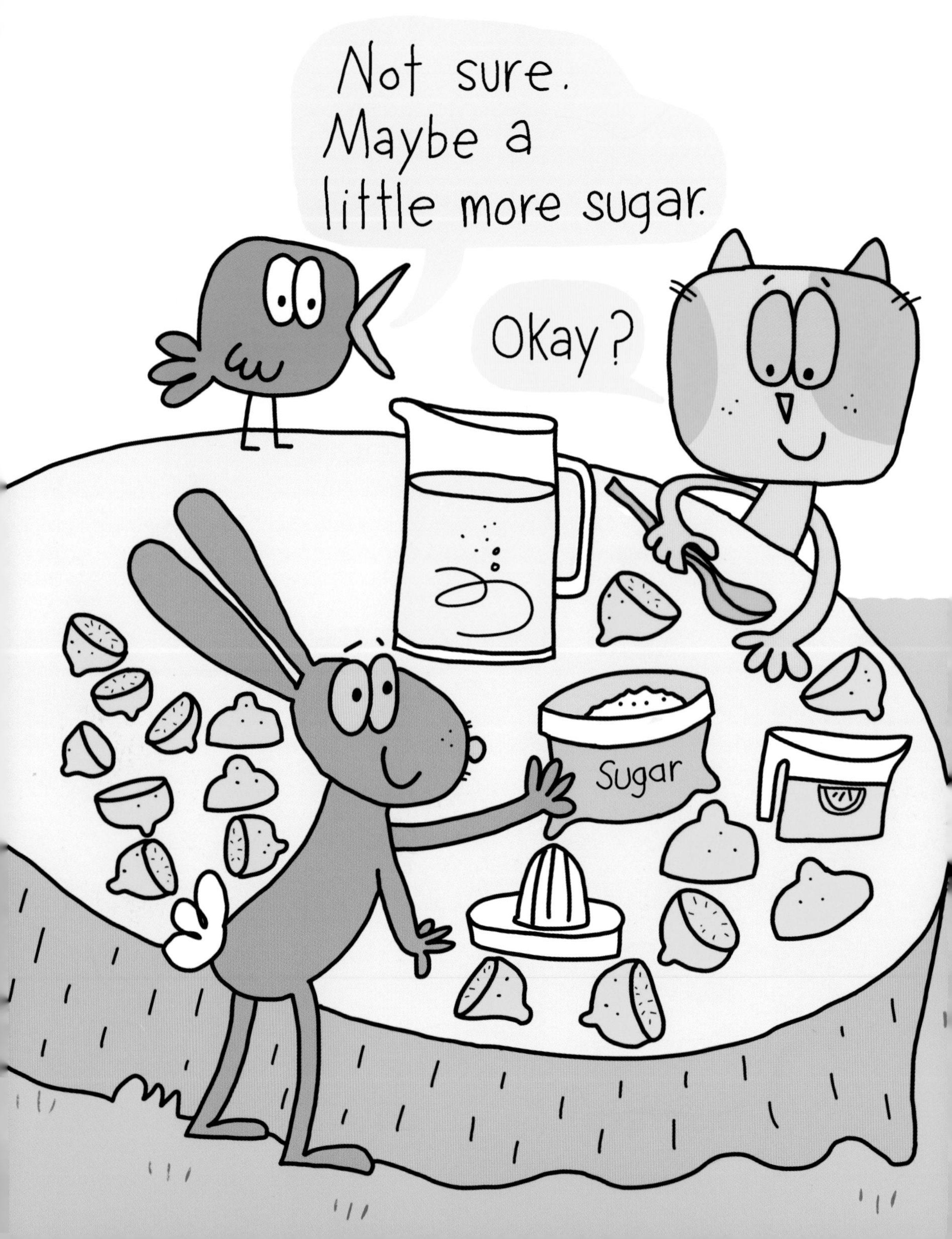
Not sure. Maybe a little more sugar.
Okay?
Sugar

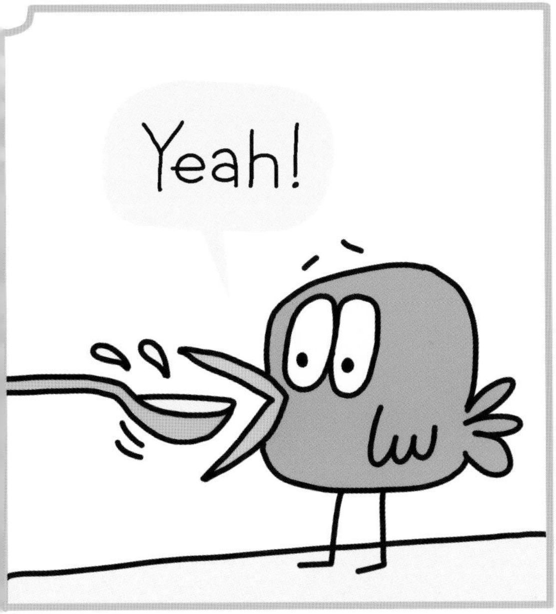
Yeah!

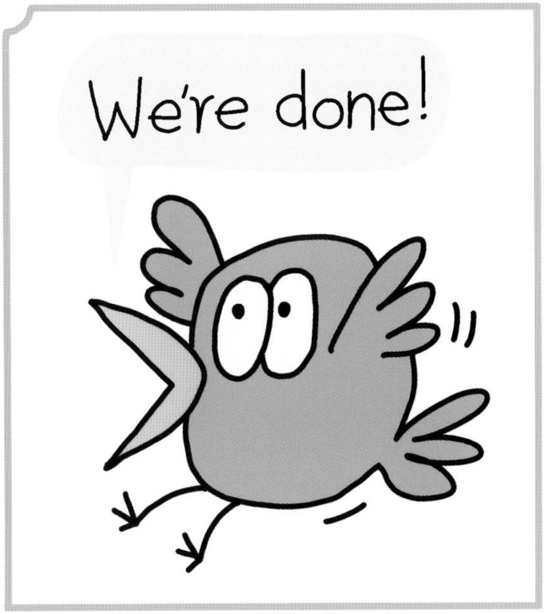
We're done!

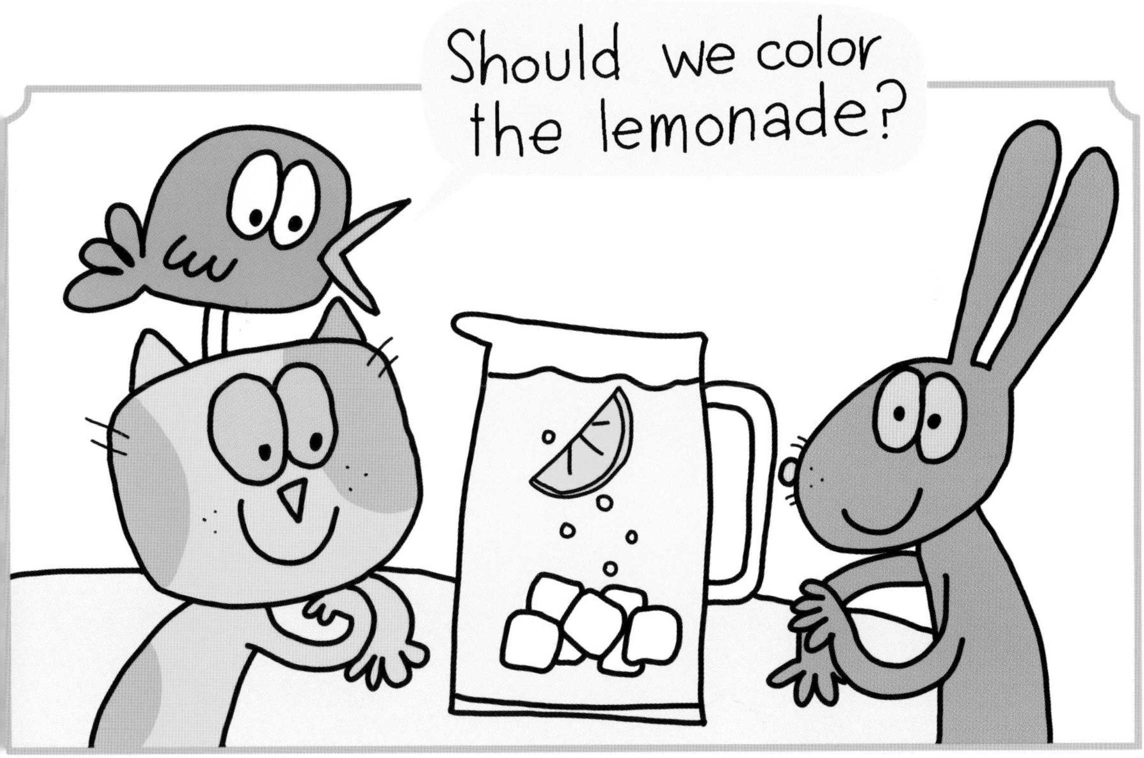
Should we color the lemonade?

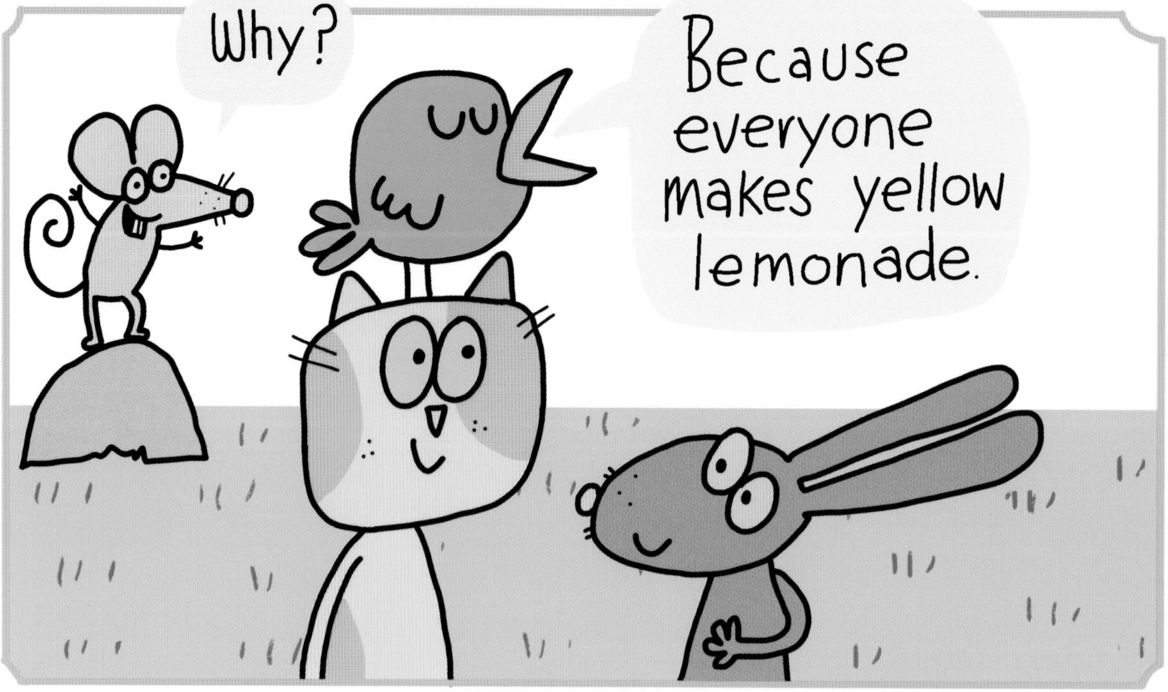
Why?
Because everyone makes yellow lemonade.

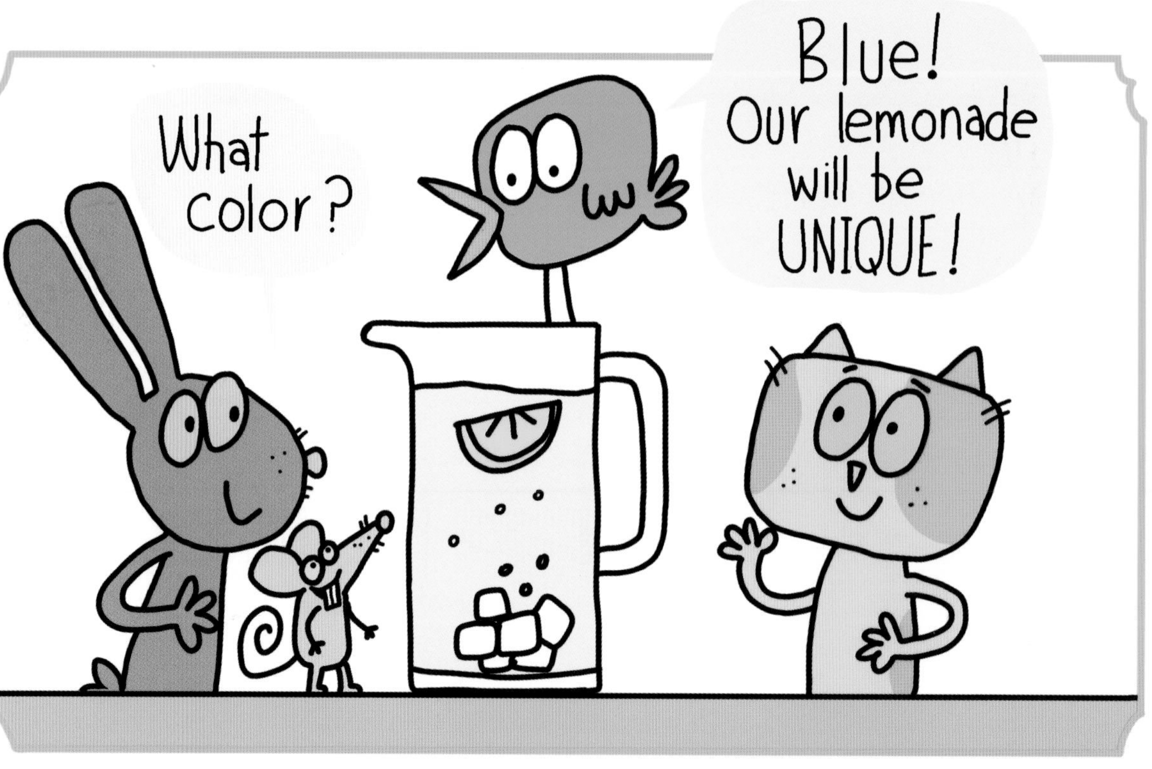
What color?
Blue! Our lemonade will be UNIQUE!

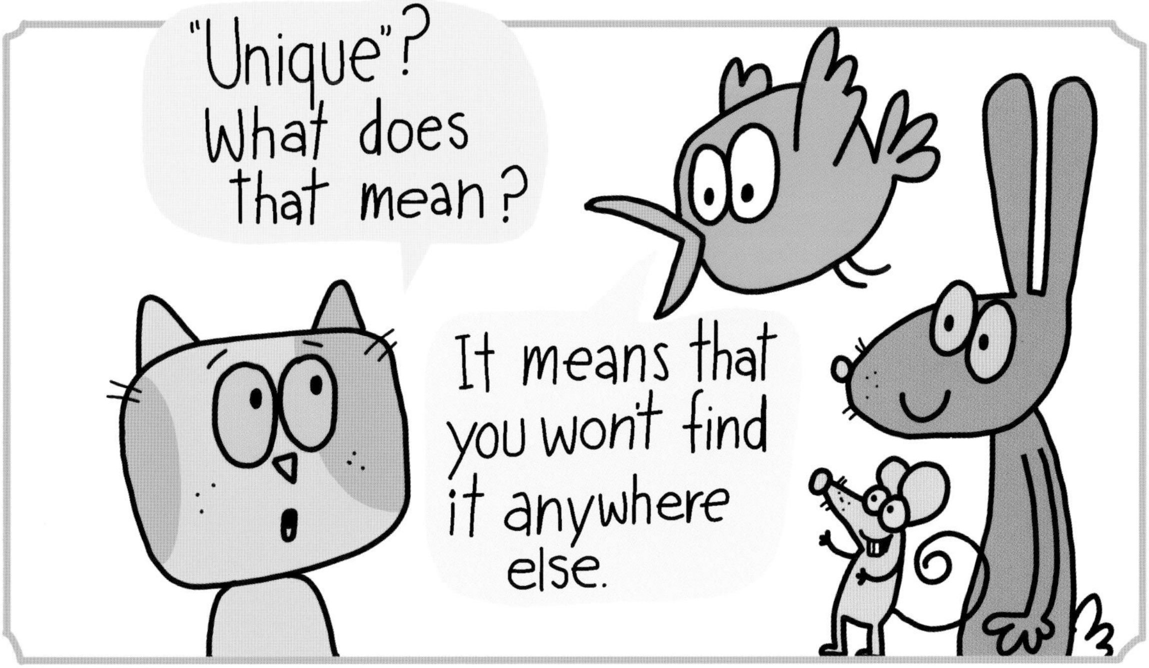
"Unique"? What does that mean?
It means that you won't find it anywhere else.

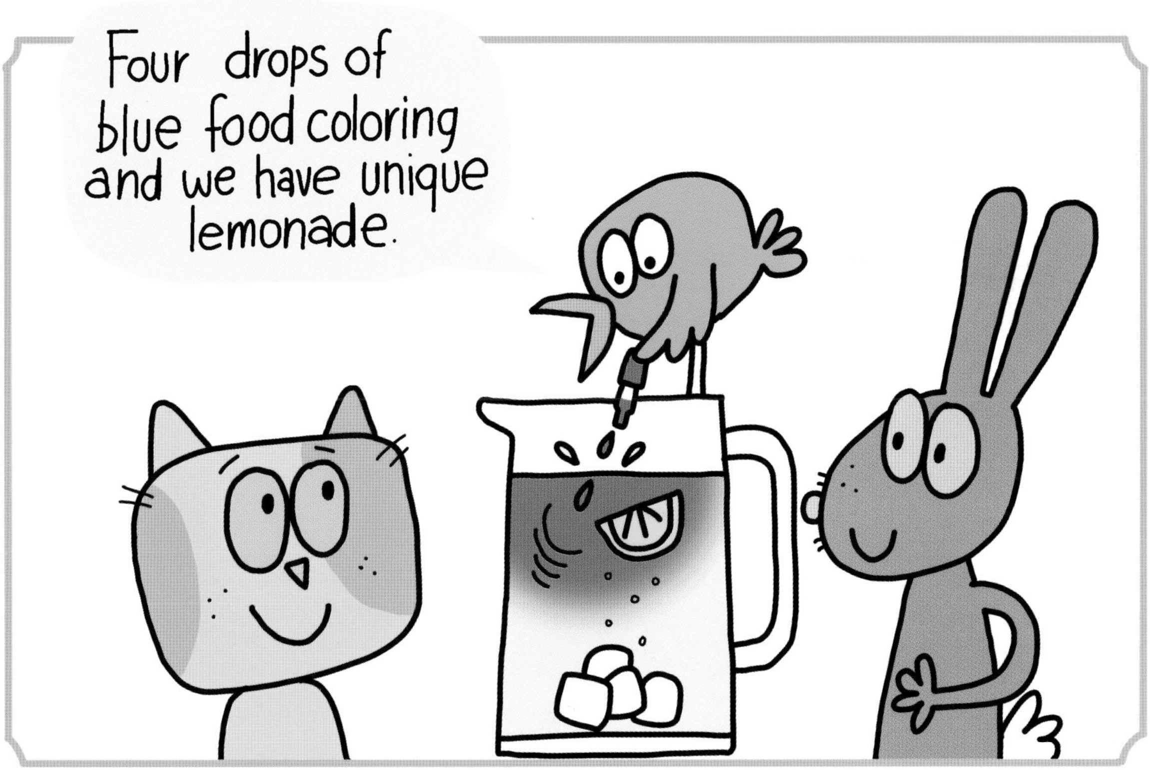
Four drops of blue food coloring and we have unique lemonade.

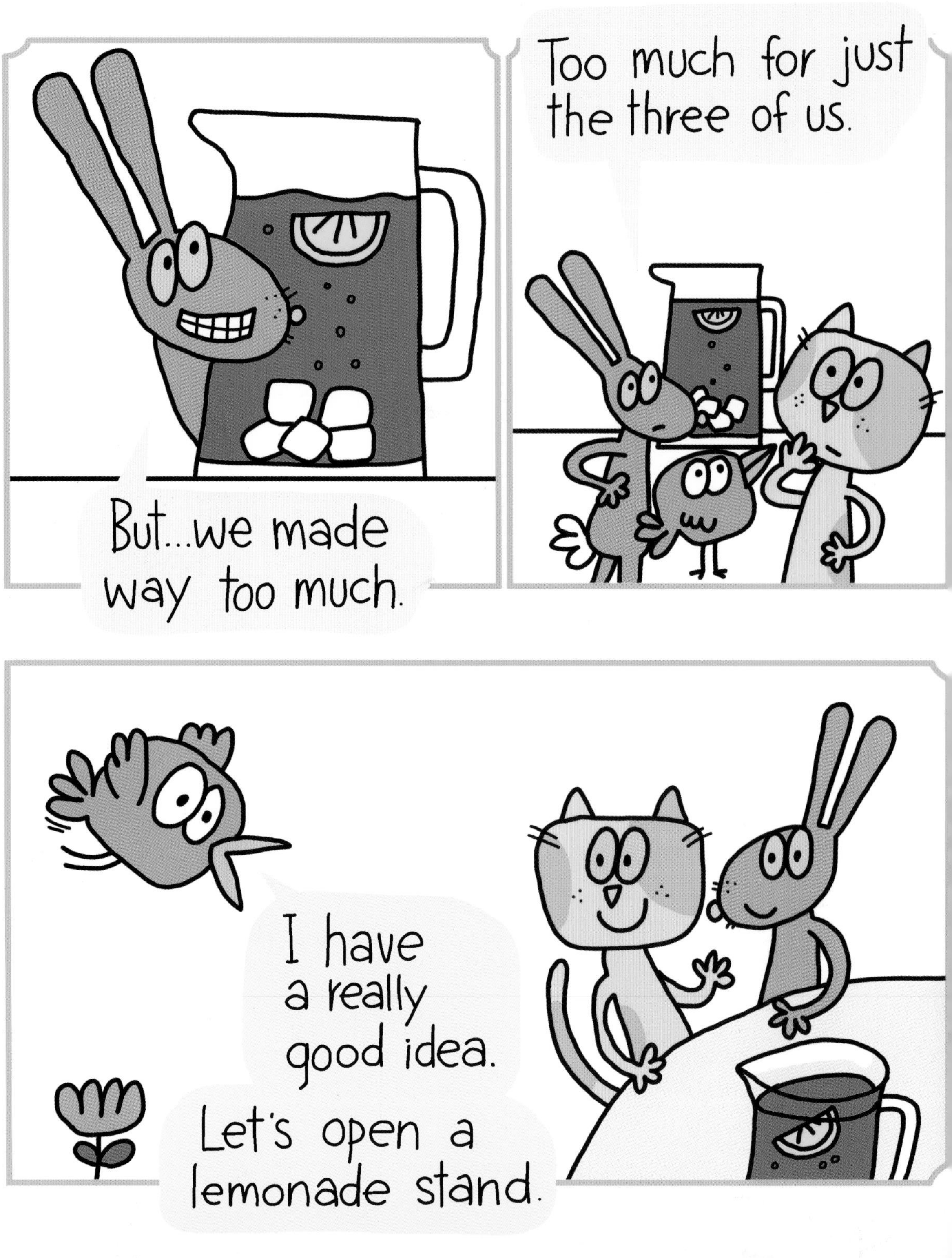
But...we made way too much.
Too much for just the three of us.
I have a really good idea.
Let's open a lemonade stand.

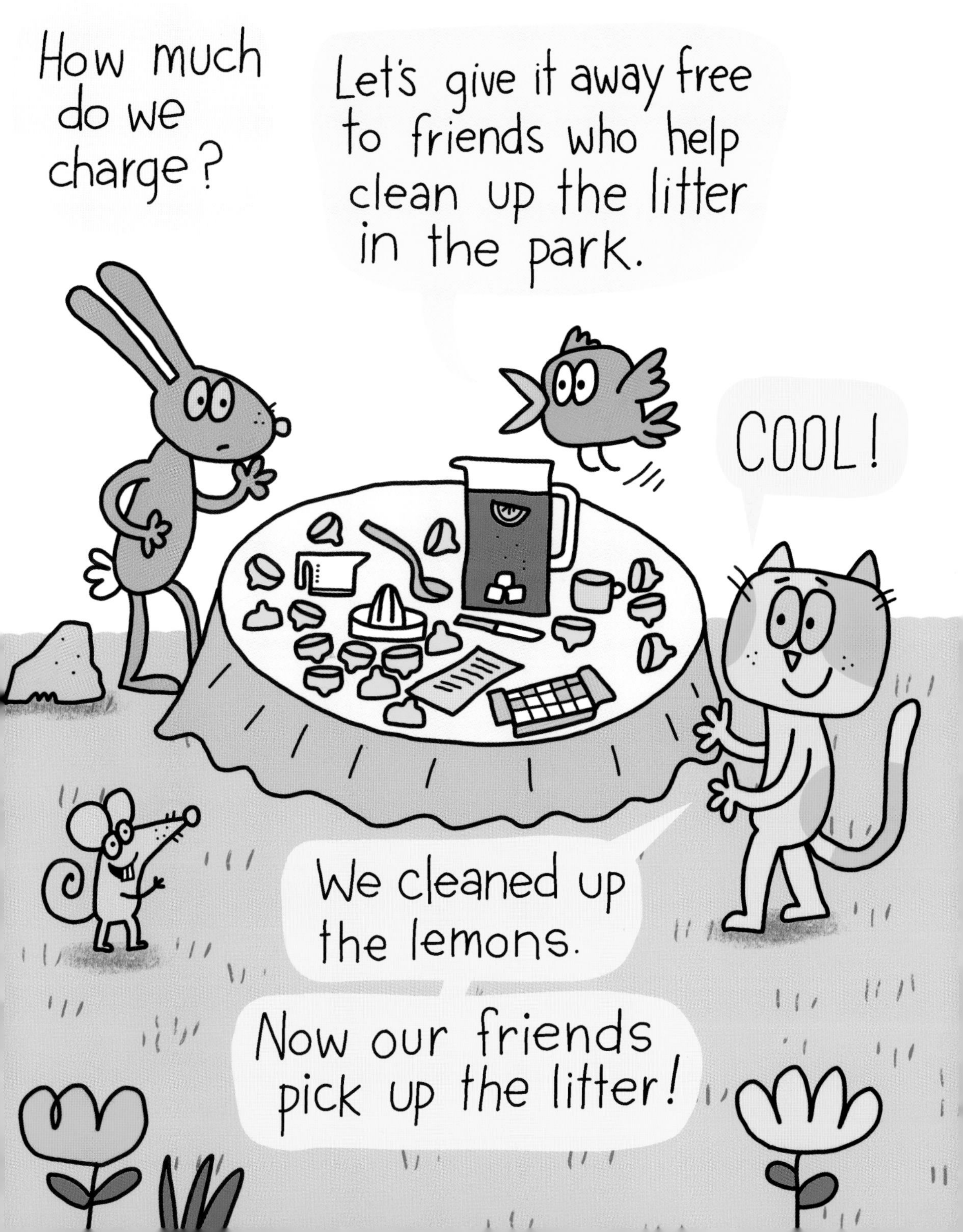
How much do we charge?
Let's give it away free to friends who help clean up the litter in the park.
COOL!
We cleaned up the lemons.
Now our friends pick up the litter!

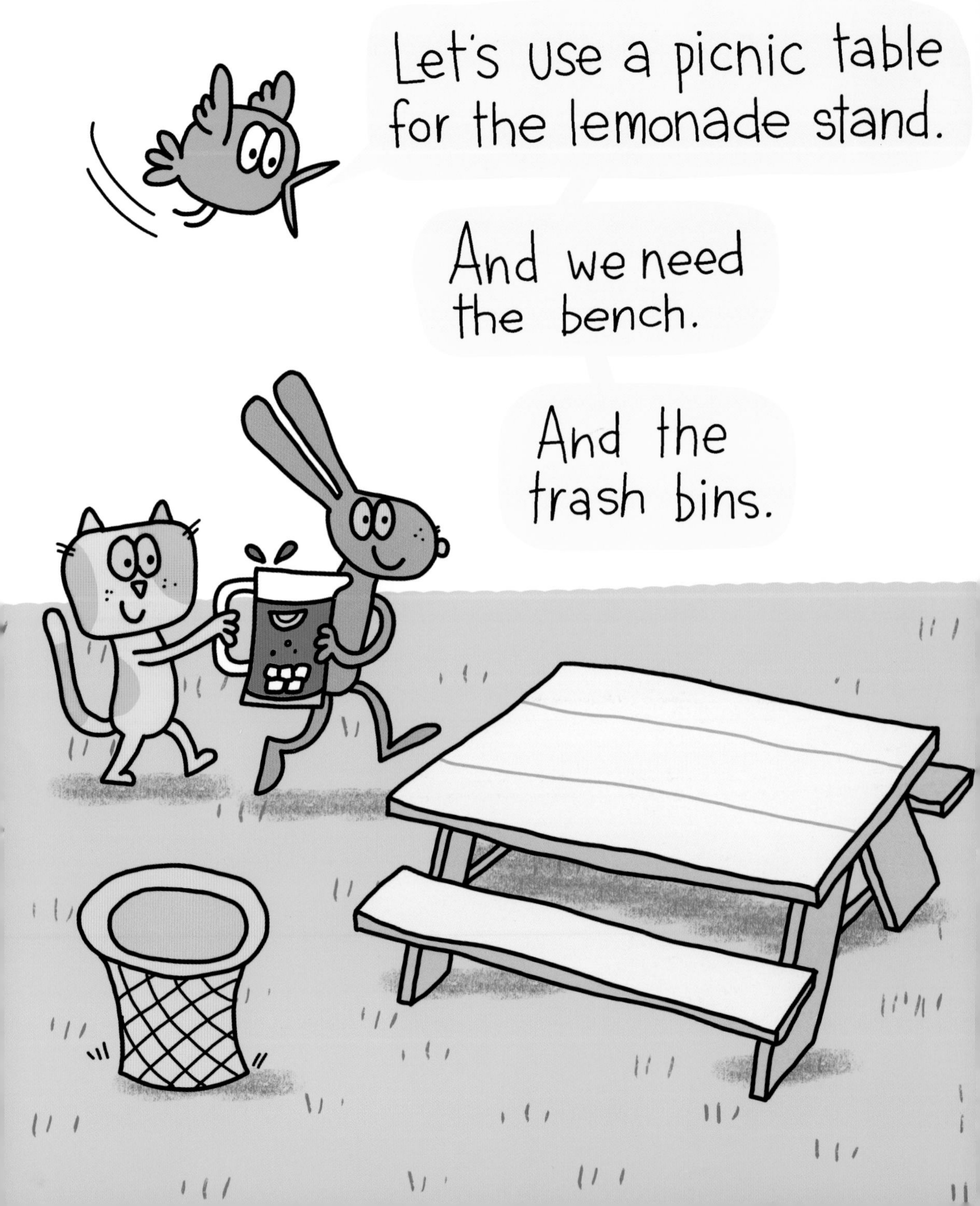
Let's use a picnic table for the lemonade stand.
And we need the bench.
And the trash bins.

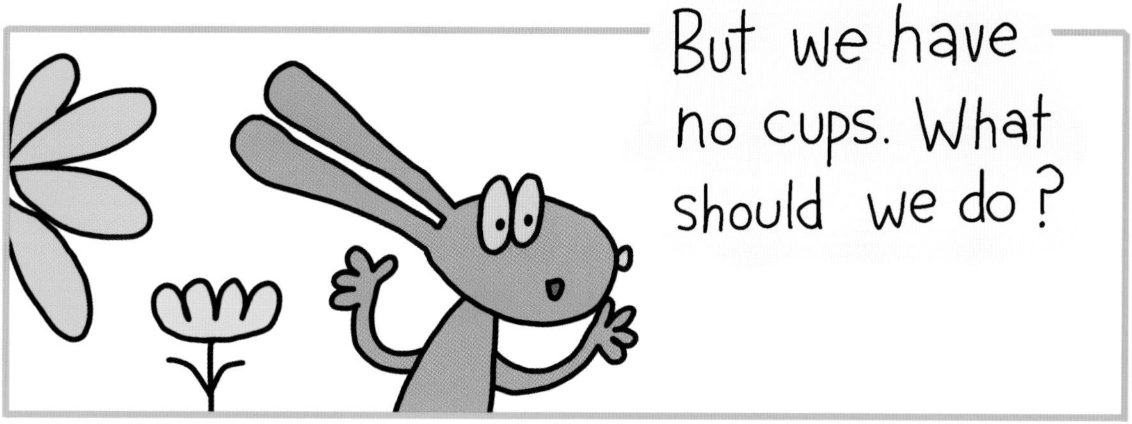
But we have no cups. What should we do?

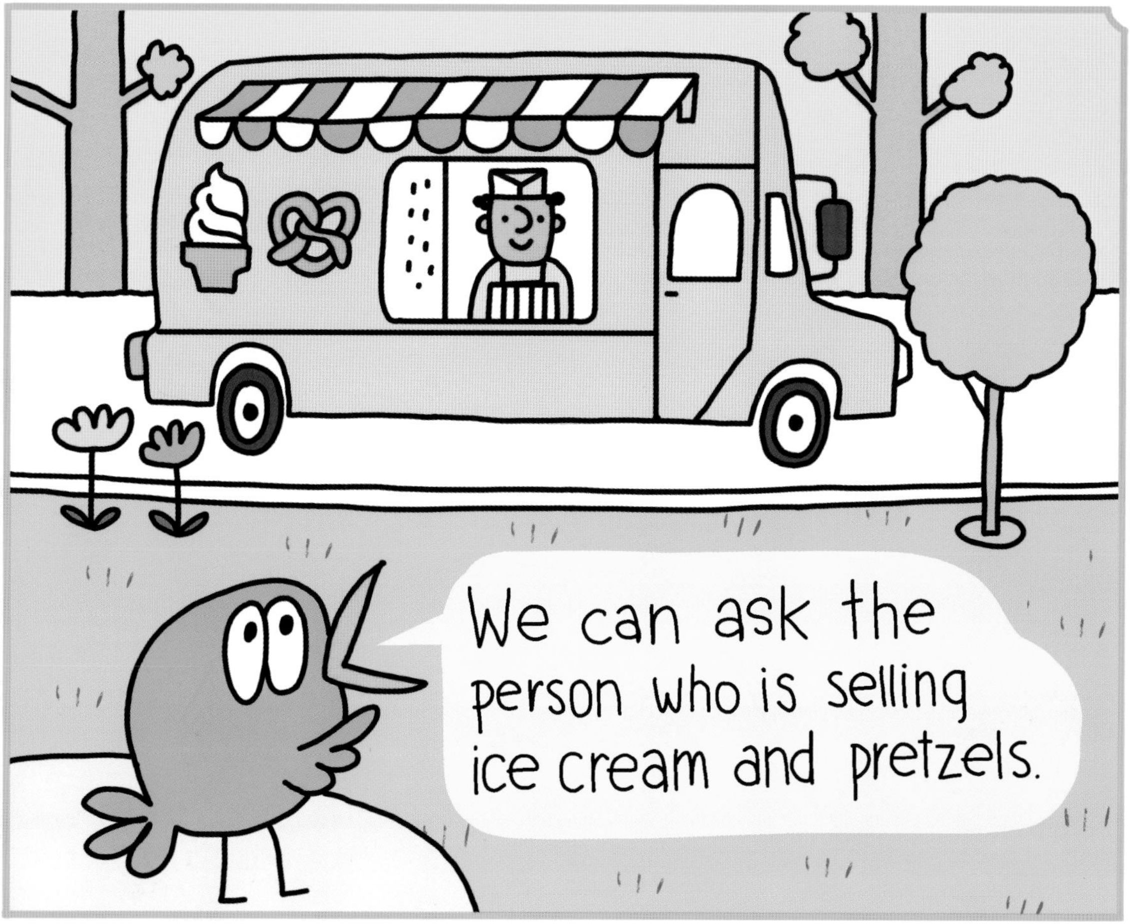
We can ask the person who is selling ice cream and pretzels.

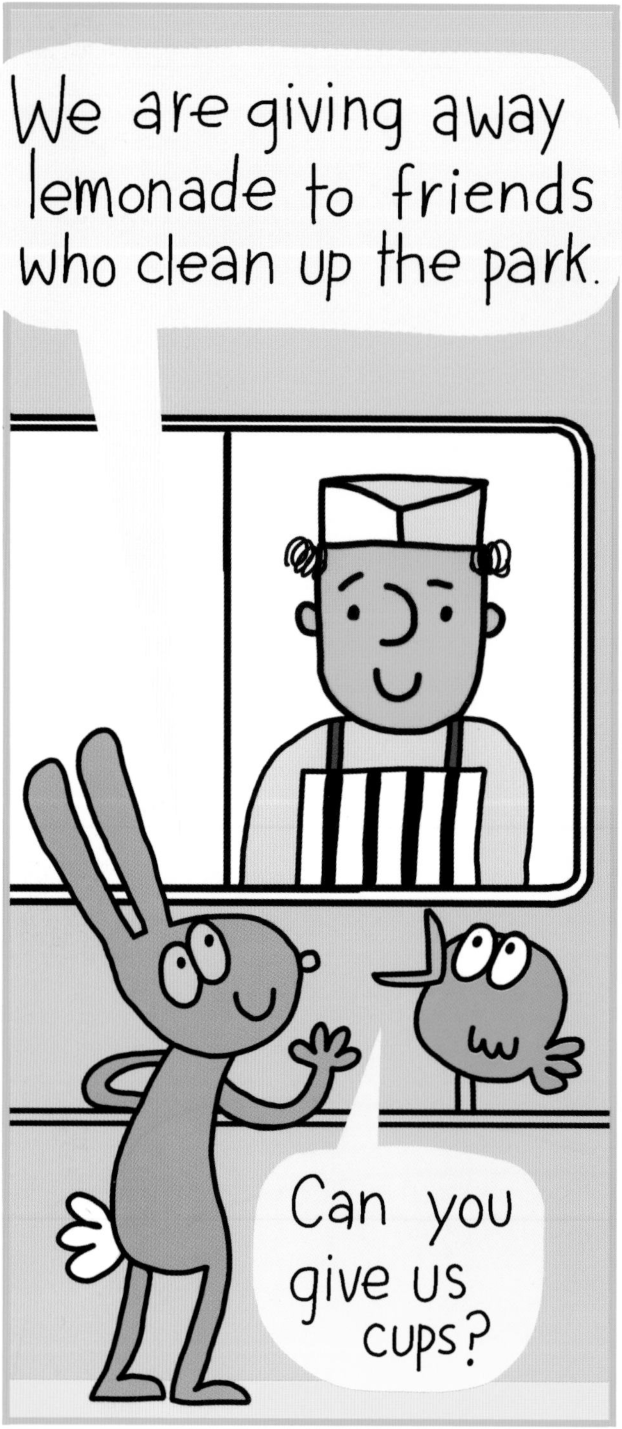
We are giving away lemonade to friends who clean up the park.
Can you give us cups?

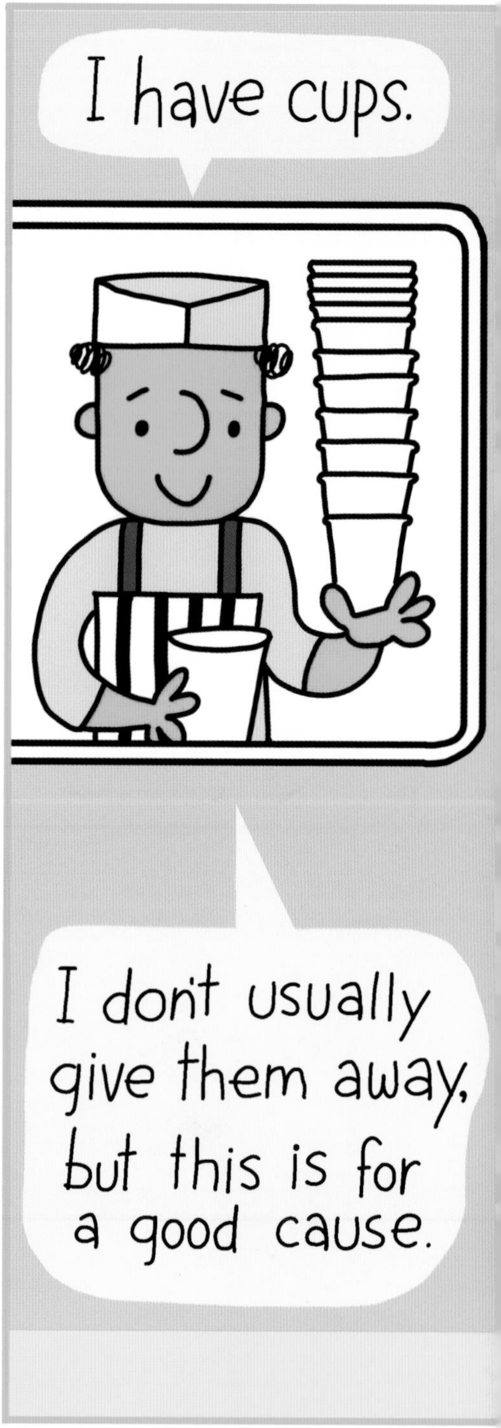
I have cups.
I don't usually give them away, but this is for a good cause.

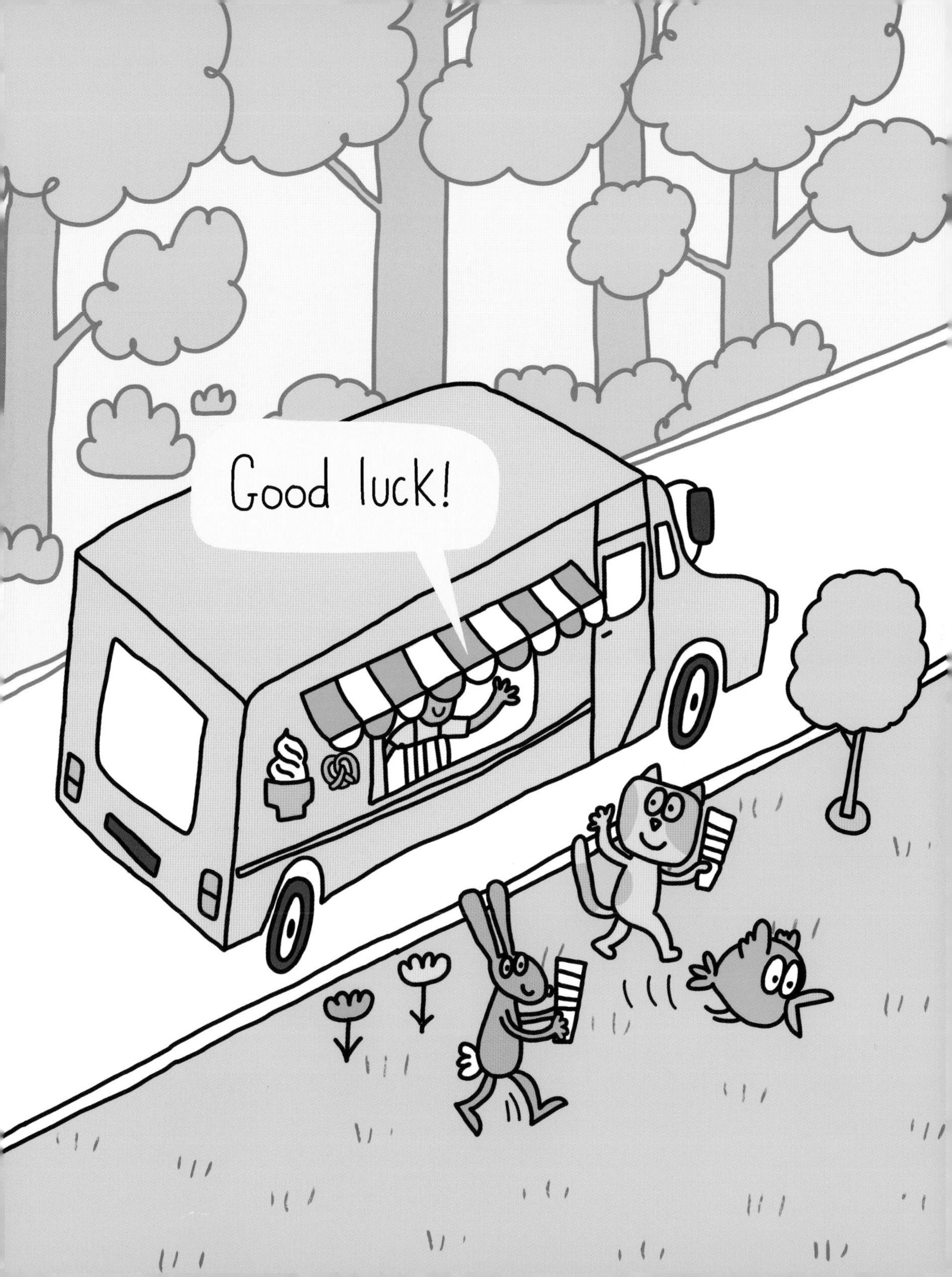
Good luck!

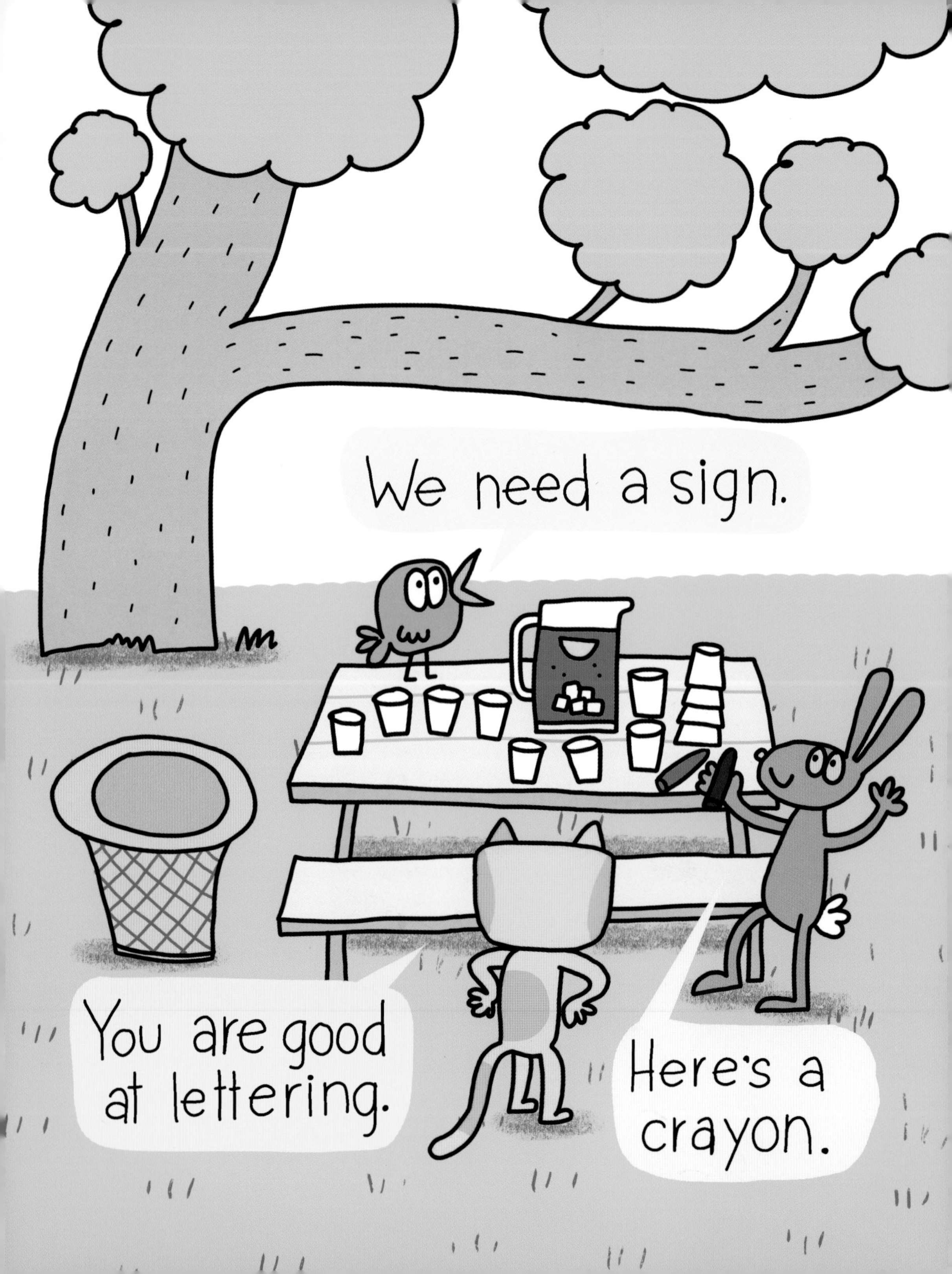
We need a sign.
You are good at lettering.
Here's a crayon.

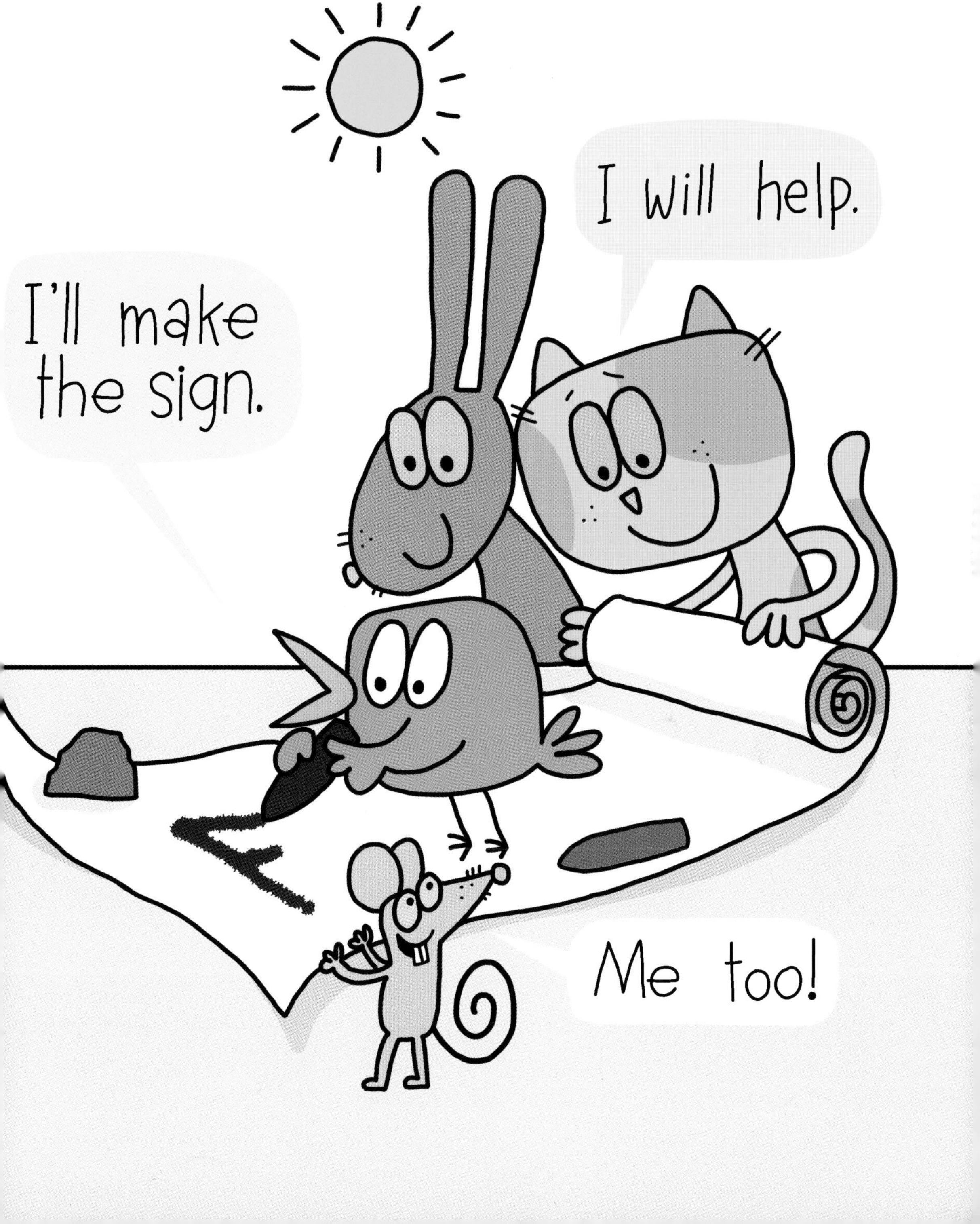

I'll make the sign.
I will help.
Me too!

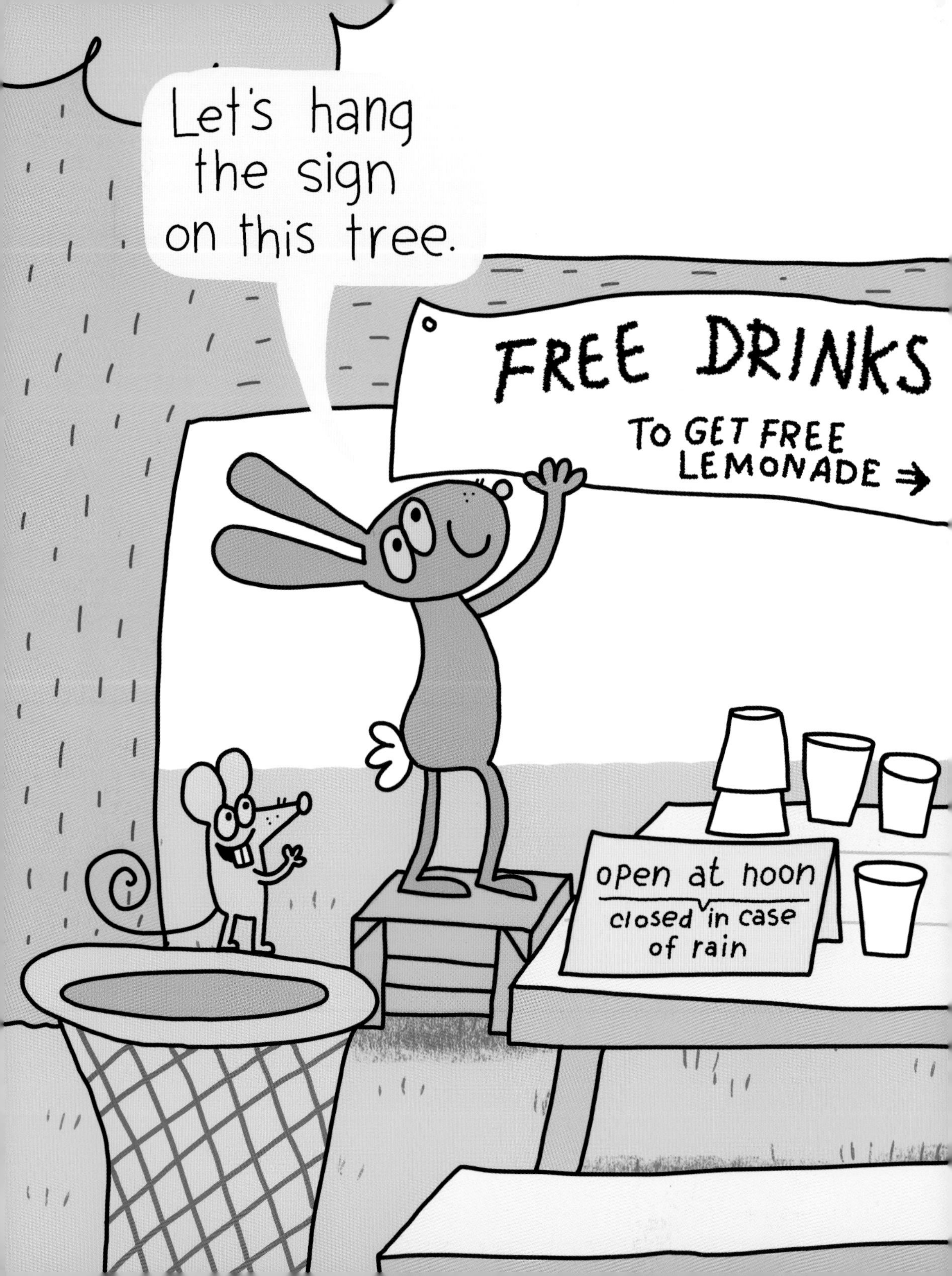
Let's hang the sign on this tree.
FREE DRINKS
TO GET FREE LEMONADE →
open at noon
closed in case of rain

BLUE LEMONADE
→ HELP CLEAN UP THE PARK
We are open!
Where are our customers?

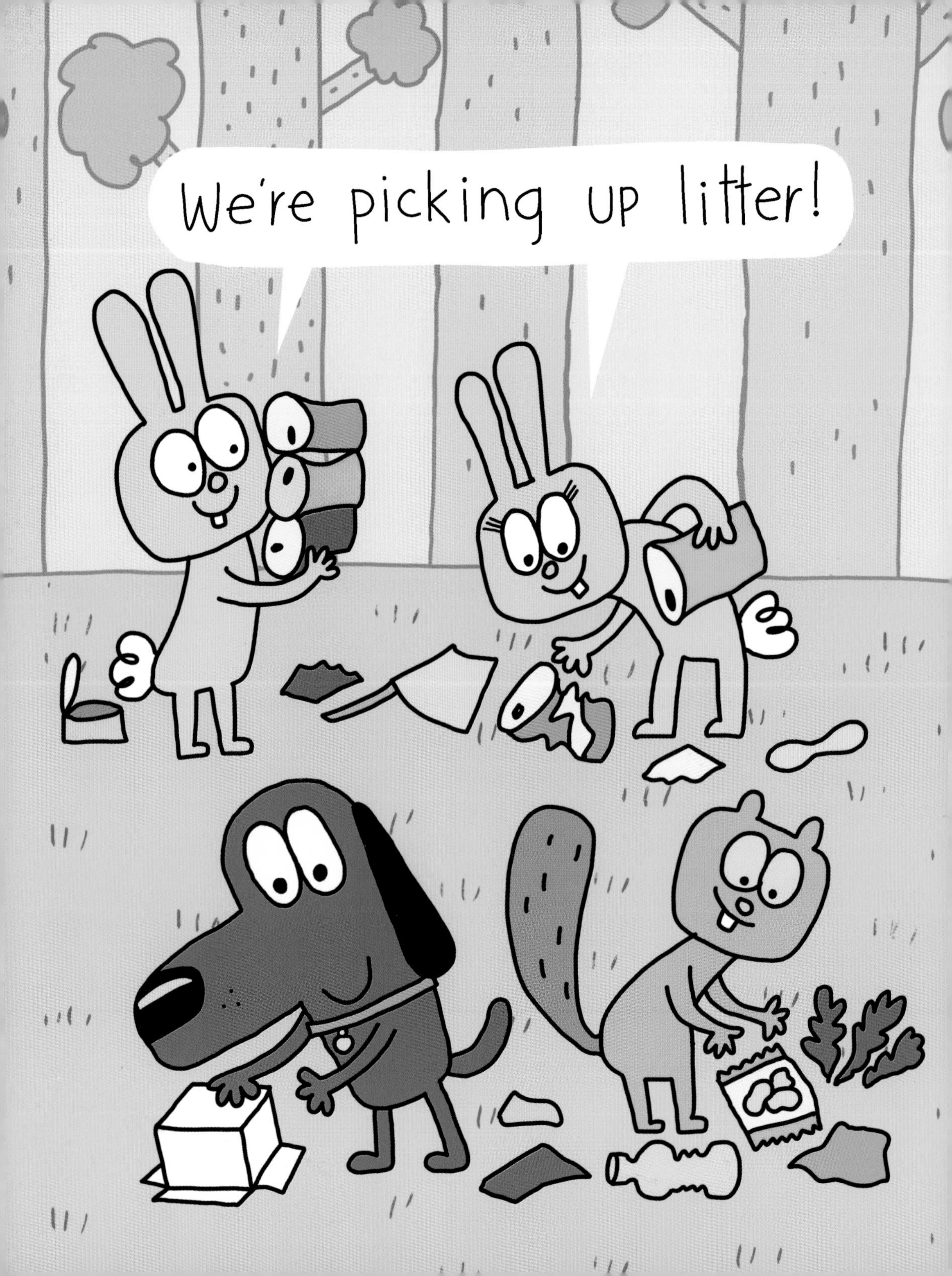
We're picking up litter!

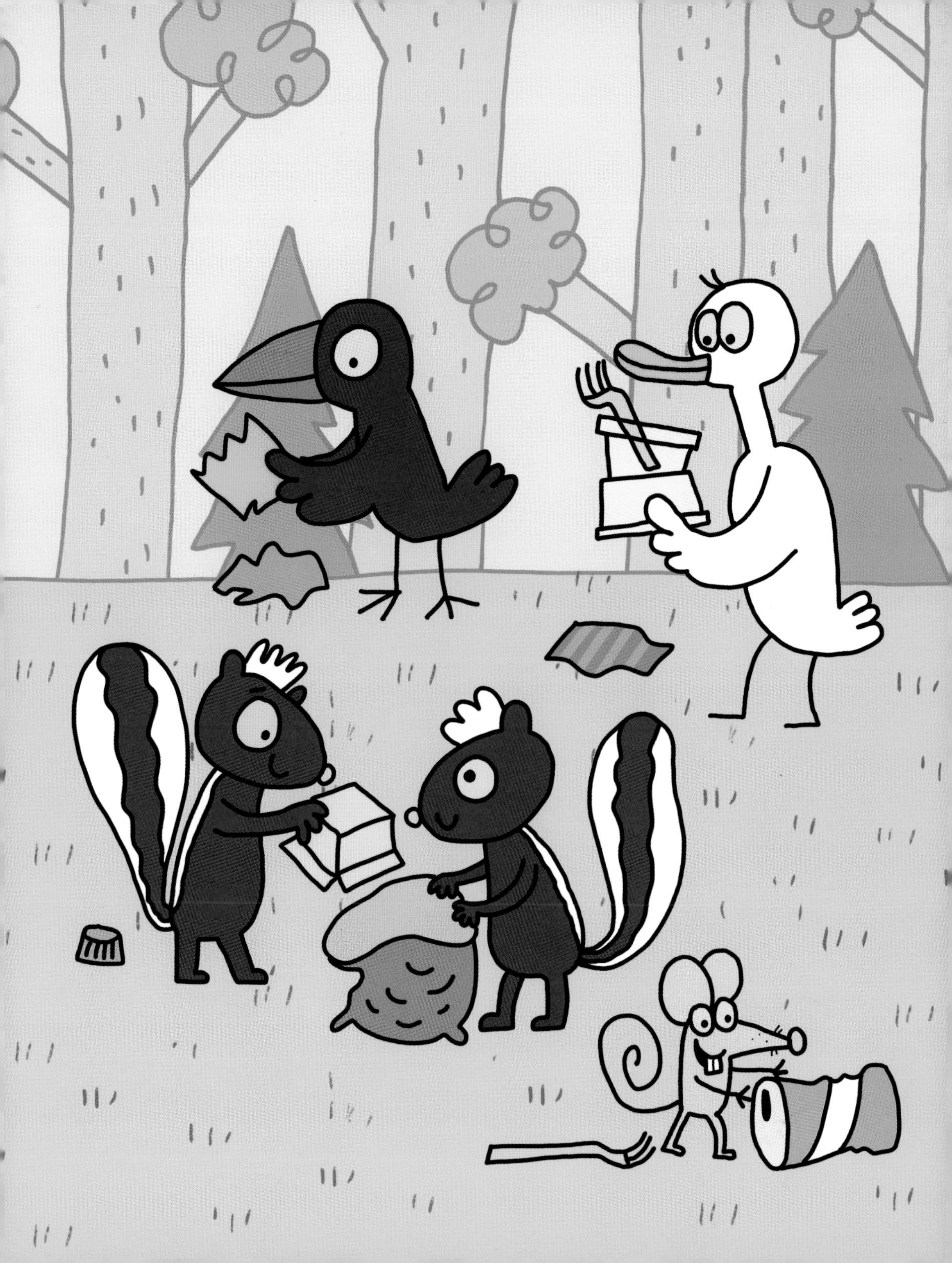

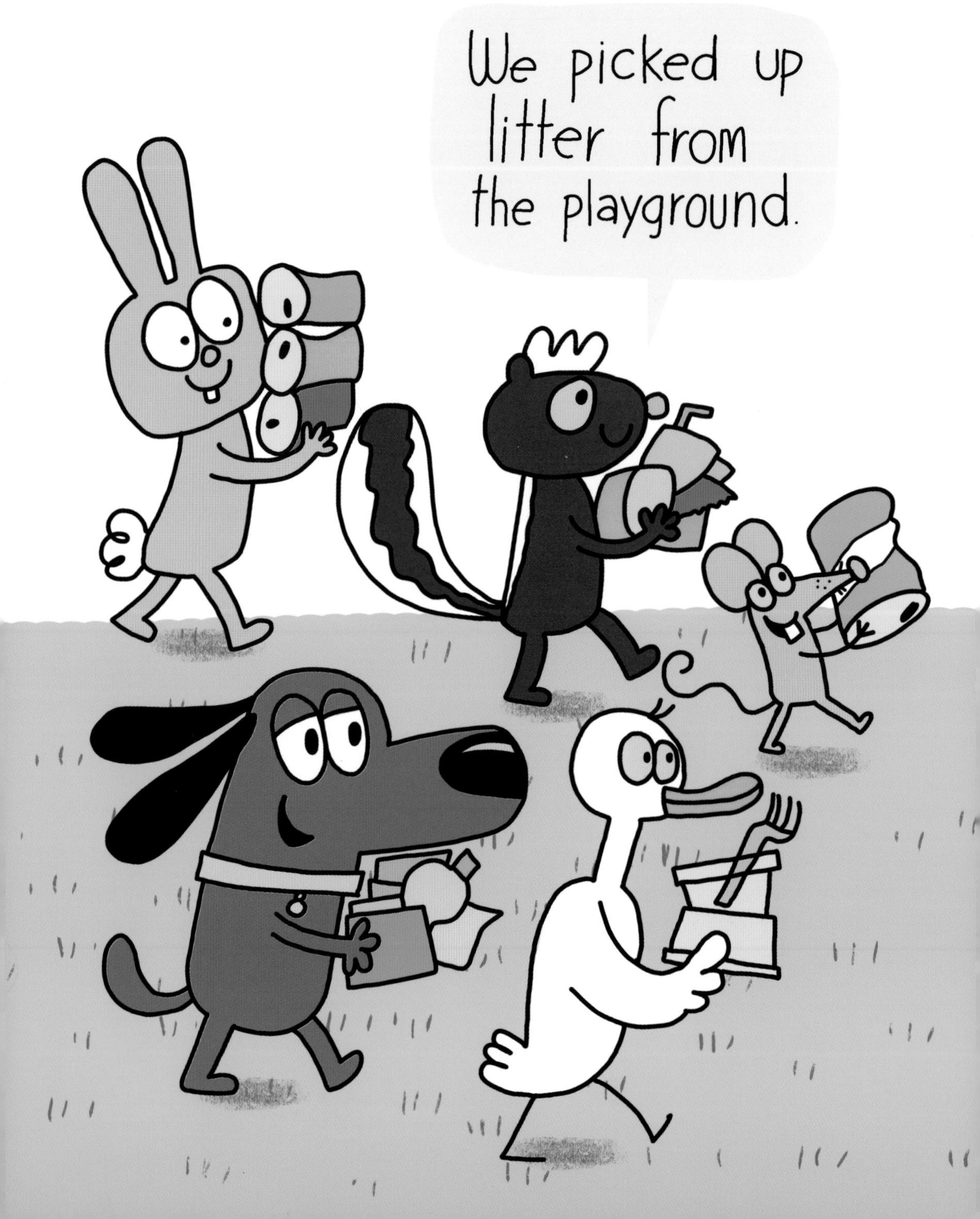
We picked up litter from the playground.

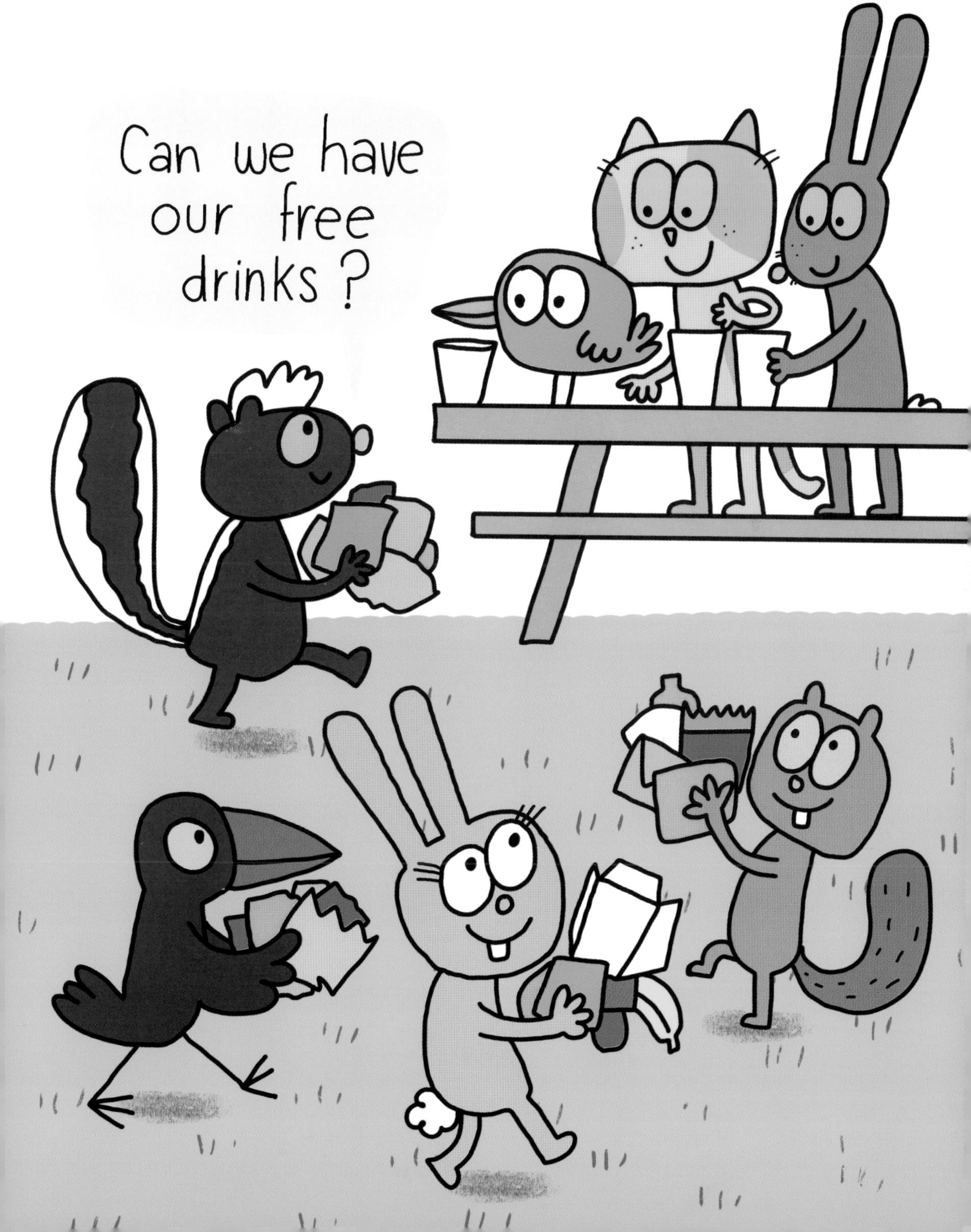
Can we have our free drinks?

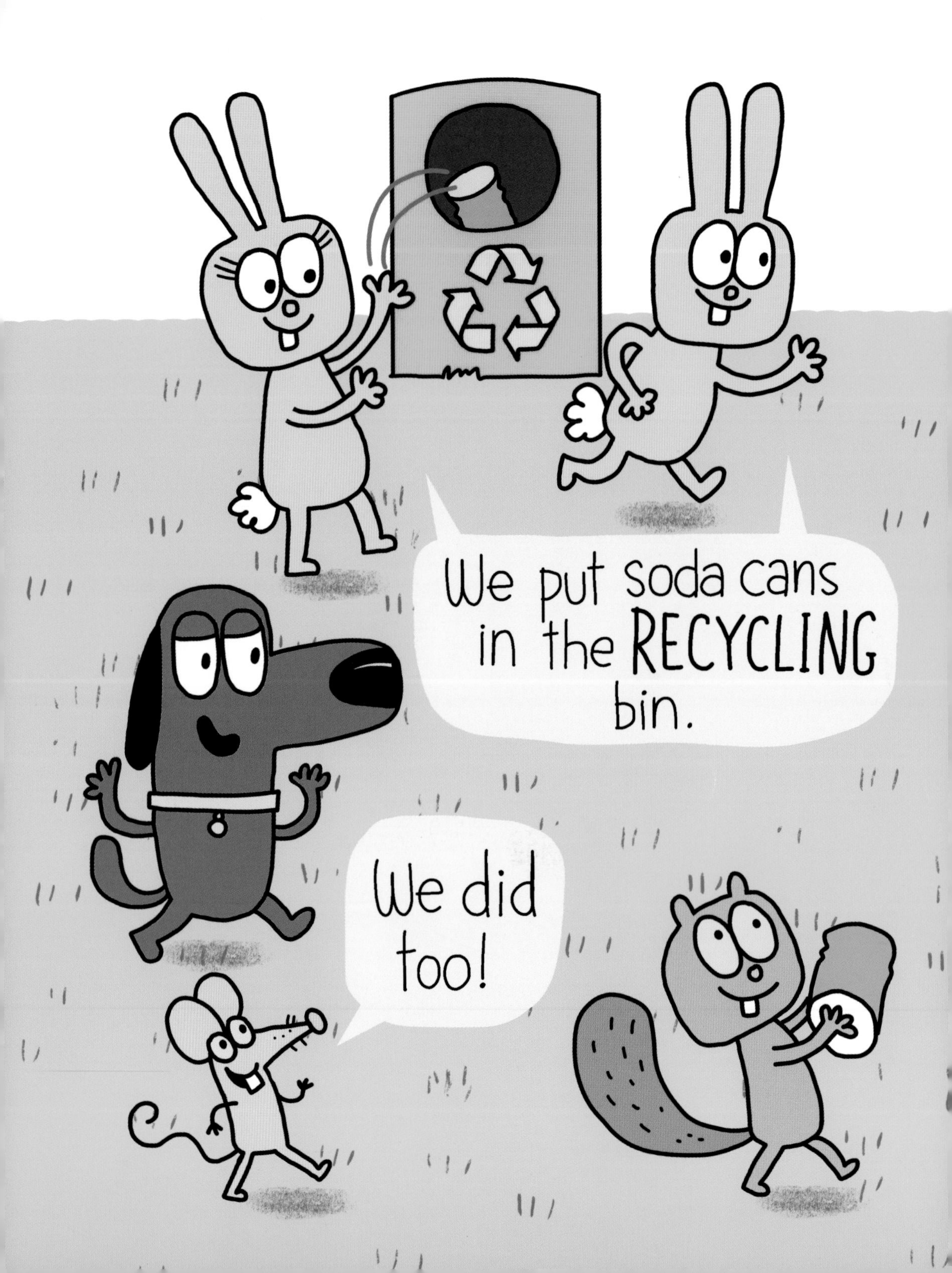
We put soda cans in the RECYCLING bin.
We did too!

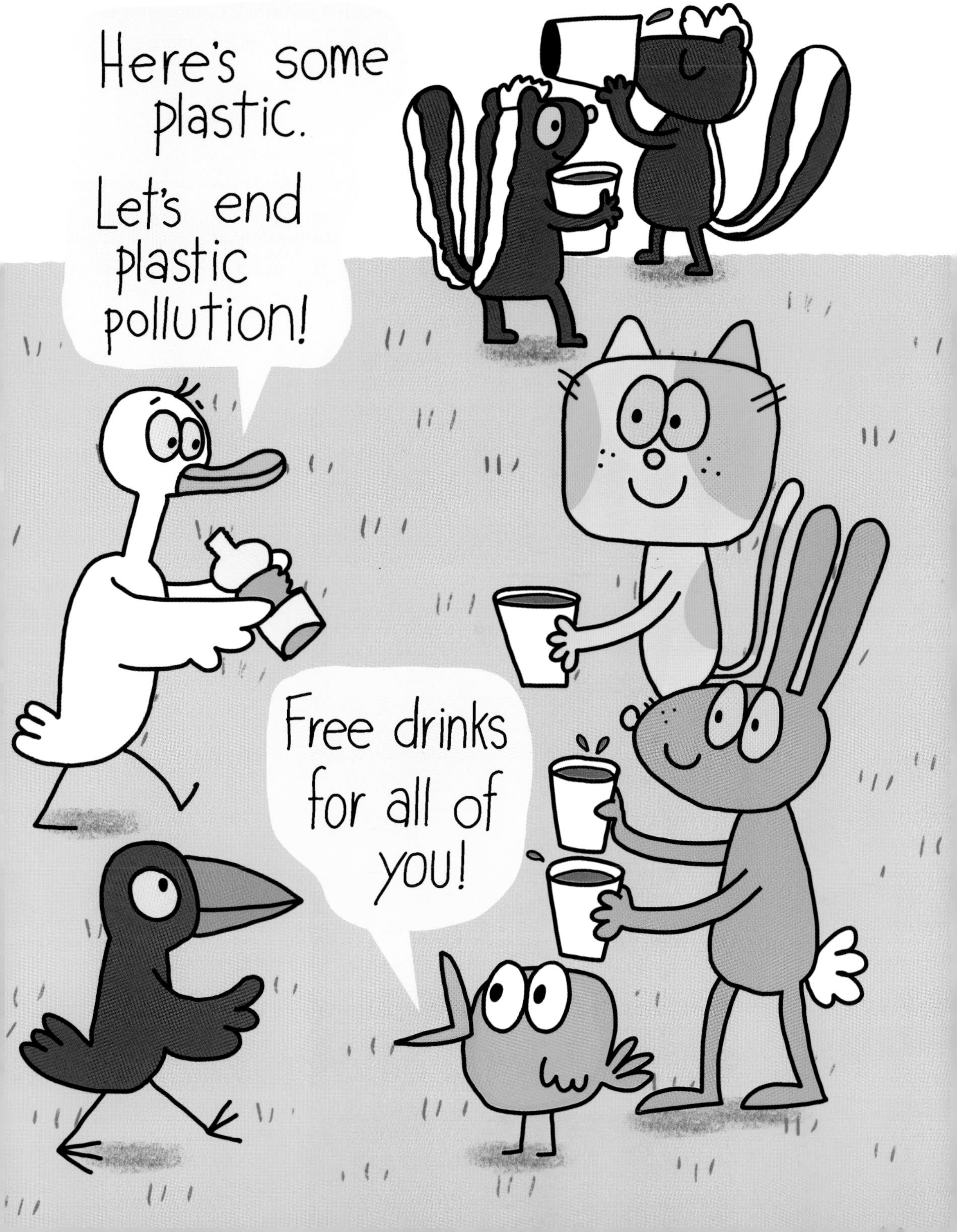
Here's some plastic.
Let's end plastic pollution!
Free drinks for all of you!

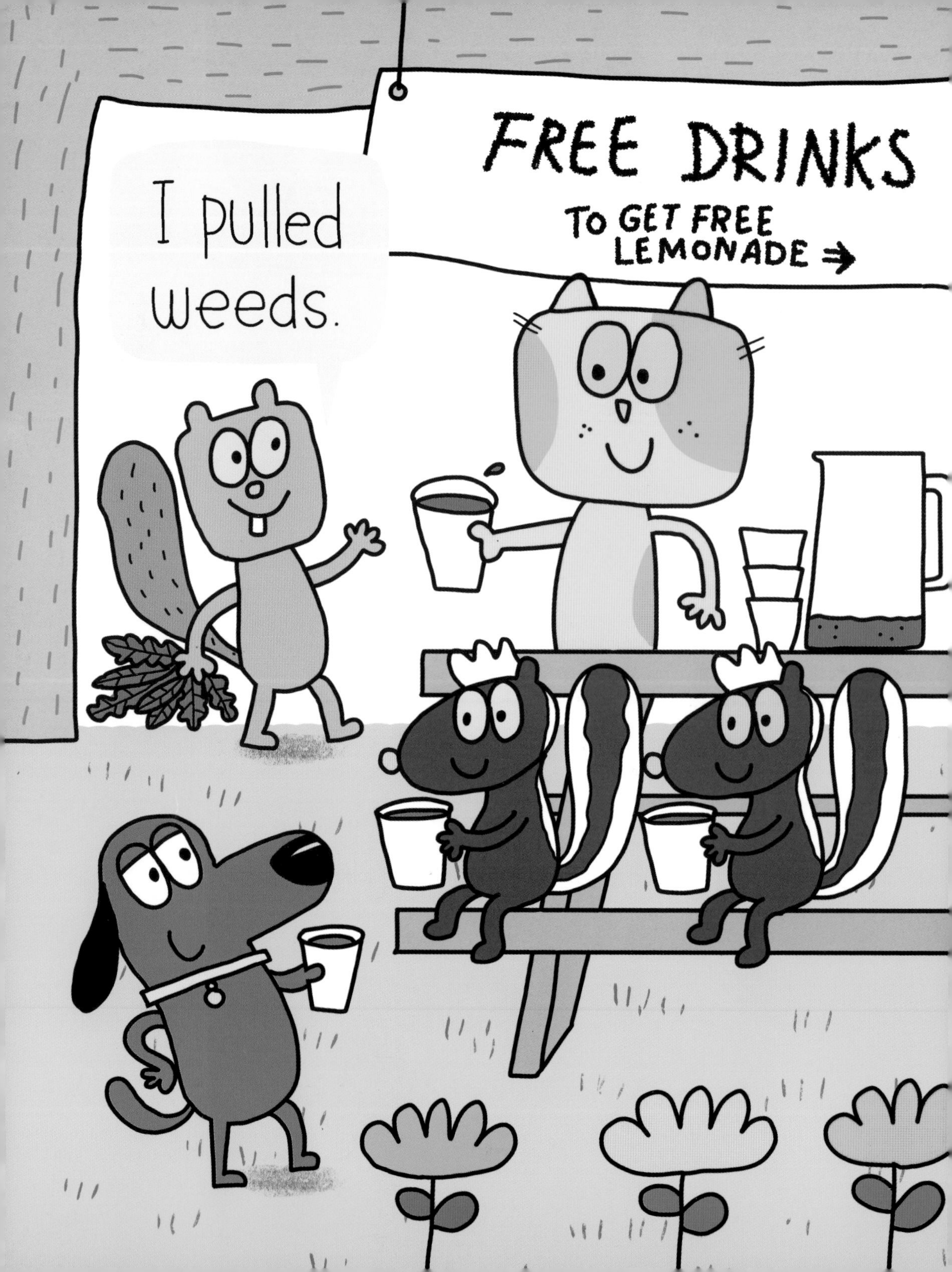
I pulled weeds.
FREE DRINKS
TO GET FREE LEMONADE →

BLUE LEMONADE
HELP CLEAN UP THE PARK
And I collected paper.
Good job!
Thank you!

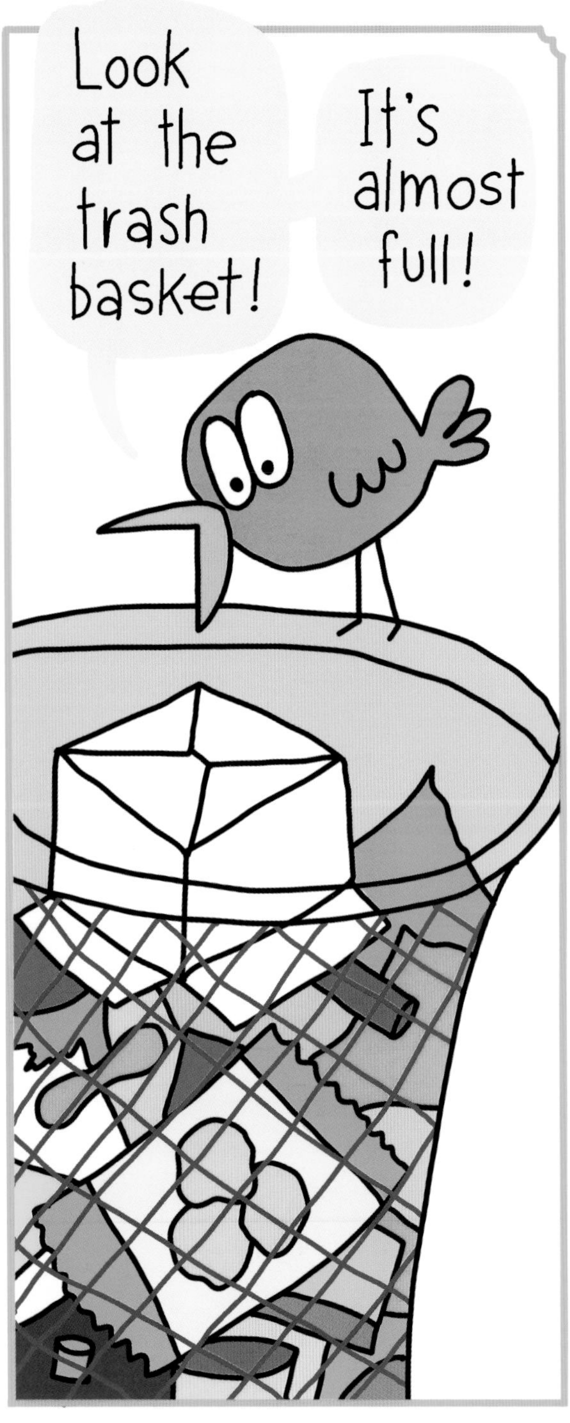
Look at the trash basket!
It's almost full!

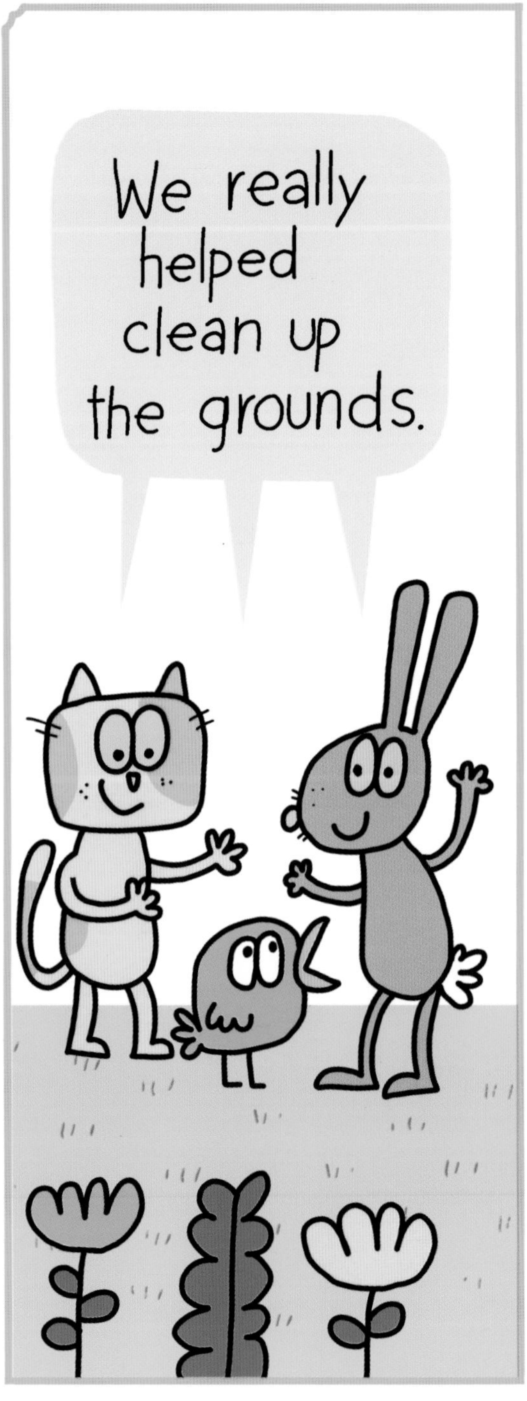
We really helped clean up the grounds.

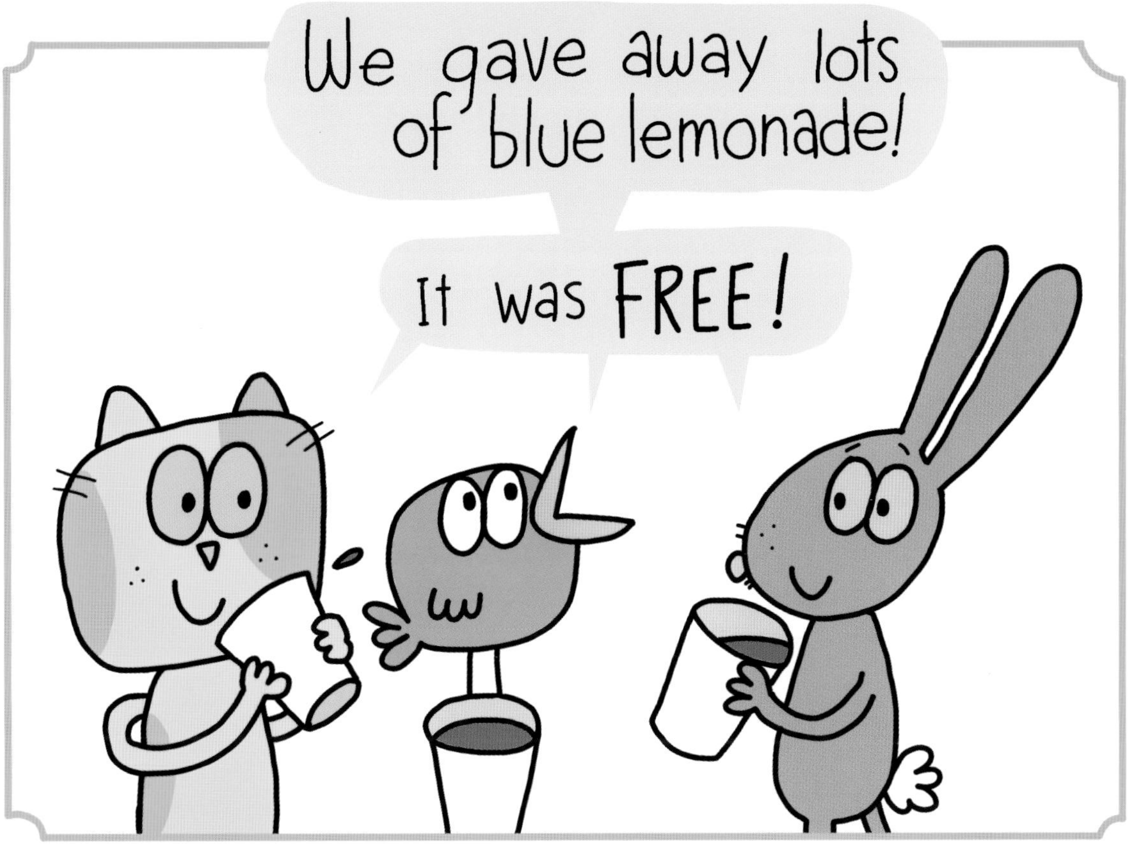
We gave away lots of blue lemonade!
It was FREE!

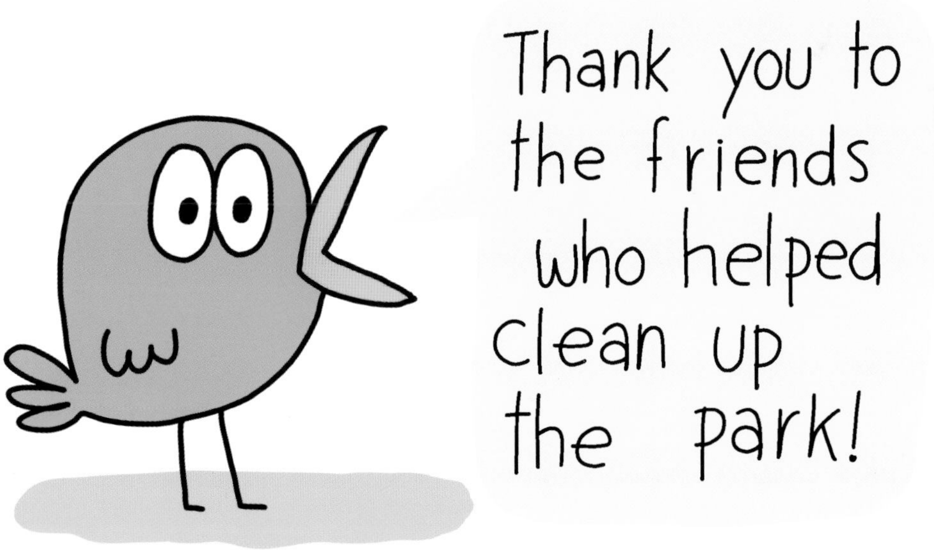
Thank you to the friends who helped clean up the park!

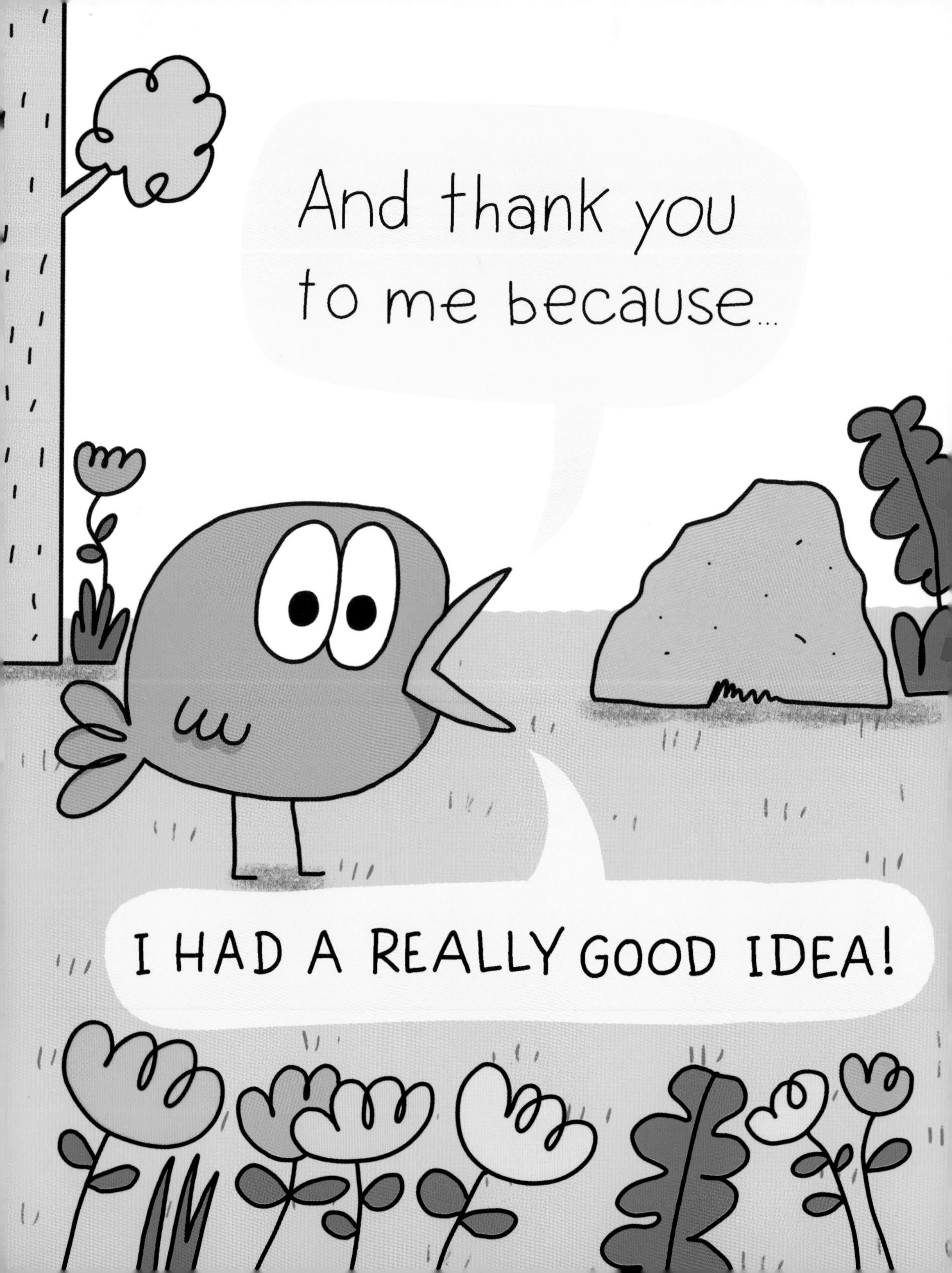
And thank you to me because...
I HAD A REALLY GOOD IDEA!

# Think About / Talk About:

- First, follow the step-by-step directions and draw Really Bird.

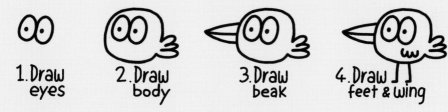

1. Draw eyes    2. Draw body    3. Draw beak    4. Draw feet & wing

- Make your own Really Bird cartoons: Really Bird sad, or hungry, or scared, or cold.

- If you had a lemonade stand, what would it look like? Draw it and make sure to include a sign and customers.

- Make blue lemonade... and share it with your friends or family. (Of course, lemonade does not have to be blue.)

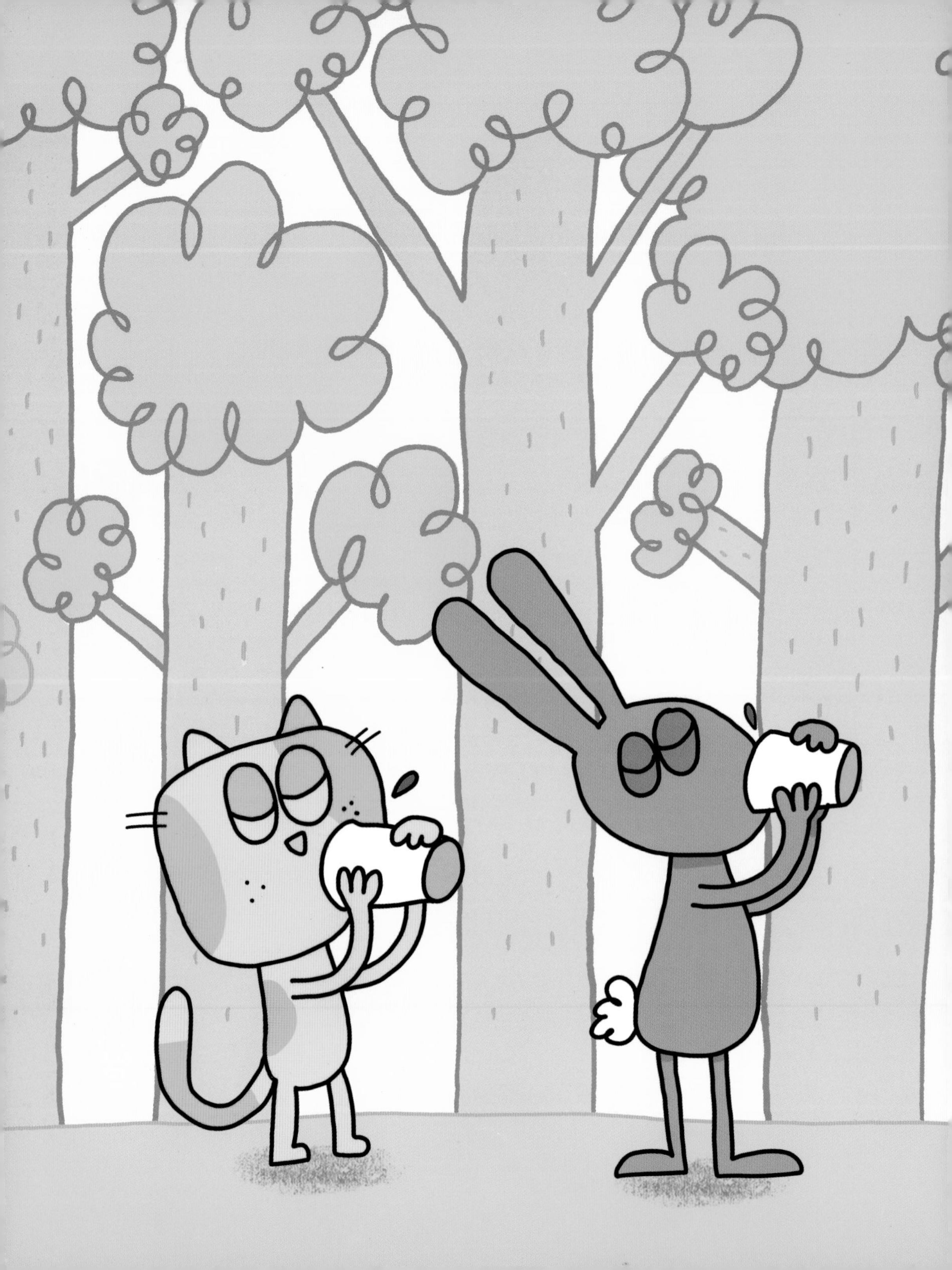